Slowly Dawn Raised Her Lashes To Look at Him.

Mixed in with the bitter pain, she could see the want that was darkening Slater's gray eyes. Her breath caught in her throat. "I was such a fool, Slater."

Eleven years of hunger were unleashed when his mouth moved onto her lips. Her fingers curled into the virile thickness of his hair. His hands were caressing, roaming at will over her back and shoulders and stirring up passions that had lain dormant for so long.

Abruptly, almost violently, Slater was pulling her arms from around his neck and pushing her from him. There was a rigid movement of his head, a negative shake that was heavy with disdain.

"You destroyed any future for us eleven years ago," he stated flatly, and started for the door . . .

Books by Janet Dailey

The Great Alone
The Glory Game
The Pride of Hannah Wade
Silver Wings, Santiago Blue
Calder Born, Calder Bred
Stands a Calder Man
This Calder Range
This Calder Sky
The Best Way to Lose
For the Love of God
Foxfire Light
The Hostage Bride
The Lancaster Men
Leftover Love
Mistletoe & Holly
The Second Time
Separate Cabins
Terms of Surrender
Western Man
Nightway
Ride the Thunder
The Rogue
Touch the Wind

Published by POCKET BOOKS

Janet Dailey

The Second Time

POCKET BOOKS

New York   London   Toronto   Sydney   Tokyo

POCKET BOOKS, a division of Simon & Schuster Inc. 1230 Avenue of the Americas, New York, NY 10020

Copyright © 1982 by Janet Dailey
Cover art copyright © 1986 Bob Maguire

Originally published by Silhouette Books.

ISBN: 0-671-69181-3

First Pocket Books printing February 1986

10 9 8 7 6 5 4 3

Map by Tony Ferrara

POCKET and colophon are trademarks of Simon & Schuster Inc.

Printed in the U.S.A.

The Second Time

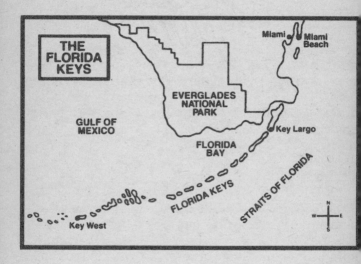

Chapter One

In the yellowing light of a May morning, it was already hot and the temperature would climb toward the hundred mark in the Florida Keys before the day was over, led by the rising sun. The quiet was broken by the droning whine of a boat's engine as it skimmed over the calm waters. The noise disturbed a pelican from its roost in the mangroves. Its lumbering bulk took wing as the skiff and its two occupants came into view.

There wasn't any breeze, but the speeding craft whipped up a wind that tore the smoke from the cigarette protectively cupped in Slater Mac-Bride's hand almost before he could taste it. Dark sunglasses were curved to his face to reduce the long glare of the angling sunlight reflecting off the water. They concealed his gray eyes, the dark color of gun metal that sometimes silvered with humor, and sometimes smoked with anger. Now they were sweeping the narrow, ever-shifting channels of the Keys' back country with calm but lively interest.

Facing into the wind, his profile was delineated by bold, sure strokes from the slant of his forehead to the straight bridge of his nose and the slight jut of his chin. A lifetime spent under a subtropical sun had tanned his skin the shade of polished teakwood and etched creases at the corners of his eyes. In contrast, the sun had lightened his brown hair, streaking its darkness with paler strands, and giving it the light and dark woodgrained look. The wind's tearing fingers had raked the hair away from his forehead and aggravated the small cowlick in the front that always gave an unruly touch to the shaggy thickness of his hair, yet not unattractively so.

The skiff sped past another island, one of the maze of coral and oolite formed islands that comprised the Florida Keys. Its shoreline was a tangle of mangrove roots, as if the trees themselves were stretching on tiptoes to avoid the sea water. At this speed, there was only a glimpse of the island and it was gone.

Ahead, Slater MacBride saw a trio of stately white herons wading along a shallow flat. Natives of these waters knew that where there were herons, it was too shallow for a boat. The weathered and decaying hull of a fishing boat that had run aground on the flat protruded from the water telling a sad tale of someone who hadn't heeded the warning of the herons' presence.

Slater was aware of the meaning of the birds but he didn't point them out to the man at the controls of the skiff. Jeeter Jones was an experienced guide, and an old family friend. He had made his living for nearly thirty years taking people sportfishing in these waters. Besides, any conversation was nearly impossible with the loud whine of the engine roaring in their ears.

Seconds later, the skiff veered slightly to the right and was aimed toward some unseen channel Jeeter Jones knew was there. The water was crystal clear, the ocean bottom plainly visible a few feet below and the depth lessening. The skiff's engine was pushed to full throttle, planing the boat to skim over the surface. Slater sat back enjoying the fast ride and the tangy sea spray on his face.

For over a hundred years, there had been a MacBride living in the Keys and working in various reputable and disreputable occupations. There had been salvage captains, not above encouraging a wreck or two, fishermen, and rumrunners, and even a relative in the cigar-making industry when it was a flourishing concern in the islands. Adaptability was almost an inbred trait. Locals said a MacBride could turn his hand and make a living at whatever enterprise was the most prosperous at the time—pity, he couldn't save any of it.

Once it had been said about Slater MacBride, too. But ten years ago, all that had changed. Now he was something of a local tycoon, owning prime business property in Key West, a couple of tourist resorts, and a small fleet of shrimp boats. A few of them knew about the girl he'd loved and lost when she chose a wealthy Texas millionaire over him. The scars and bitterness were on the inside; the hurt had gone too deep to ever be truly erased.

As the skiff neared the basin, the engine was

throttled back to almost idling speed. The air stopped its rush and became still, like the flat, slick surface of the water glistening in the sun and blending into the blue sky.

"This here's the place." Jeeter Jones cut the engine and picked up the fiberglass push pole to quietly enter the basin. Late May was the season when the tarpon were abundant and moving. It was the lure of this game fish that had drawn Slater away from his varied business interests, a rare break for him nowadays. "Think you still know how to catch one?" Tufts of graying hair poked out from beneath his sun-and-sea-softened captain's hat. Its texture was wiry as if permanently stiffened by years of salty air.

"You find me one and put me in casting distance, and we'll find out," Slater replied dryly to the challenge to his infrequently used skill.

"Old Pop Canady was down at the marina yesterday afternoon. Did I tell you?" Jeeter expertly poled the skiff into the basin, barely making any noise at all.

"No." Slater no longer stiffened at the mention of the name Canady, but there was an inner resistance, a tightening of nerves.

The guide sent a brief, skimming look at the thirty-five-year-old man he'd known since boyhood, so he was more aware than most of the startling contrast from the devil-may-care young man to the successful entrepreneur sitting in his boat. Most people thought Slater had gotten over what had happened eleven years ago, but Jeeter wasn't so sure. He'd played poker with the man too many times to believe his hard, smooth features weren't hiding something.

If he was right, then Slater deserved to be told the news so he could be prepared for it. And if he was wrong, it would be like water rolling off a duck's back. It wouldn't matter.

"Yeah, Pop was all puffed up and bragging. It seems Dawn is coming home, so he'll be bringing his grandson around to show him to all his friends." Out of the corner of his eye, Jeeter caught the sharp glance Slater threw him, although nothing flickered on his deadpan expression.

"I imagine Pop would be happy about that." Slater managed a noncommittal response and contained any reaction to the disruptive announcement.

Inwardly he was damning the cruelty of his mind that wouldn't let him bury the past. If he closed his eyes, he knew he'd recall the sweet scent of gardenias, waxen white against flaming copper hair. Bitterness choked his throat. Dawn had loved him, but she had married money. At the time he'd had no future, and no prospect of any, and she had wanted more than love. He didn't blame her as much as he used to, but that didn't ease the bitterness her decision had created.

"You knew her husband died a month ago, didn't you?" Jeeter inquired in a casual voice.

"I heard." His gaze remained on the water as if

waiting for the first glimpse of a tarpon's wide oily back rolling out of the water, but he was seeing nothing. "She's coming back a very wealthy widow. Will she be arriving by yacht or a private jet?" A bitter sarcasm was threaded through his taut voice despite his attempt to keep it in check.

"Pop never said," Jeeter admitted, referring to Dawn's father. "I always got the feeling her husband didn't want her having anything to do with her parents, like they wasn't good enough for the likes of him, even if he did marry their daughter. He never did bring her back to visit after they got married."

For his sake, Slater had been glad Dawn had left and not come back. There was a time when he had been driven wild by jealousy at the thought of her lying in Simpson Lord's arms after she'd been in his. It still pained him to remember that last night together when they had made love till morning. He had been so certain that she couldn't love him and leave him after that.

Yet she had dressed and calmly slipped that huge diamond sparkler on her ring finger, reaffirming her intention to marry the wealthy Texan, even though she didn't love him. Until that moment, he had been prepared to believe that her young, eighteen-year-old head had been briefly turned by the gifts and attention Simpson Lord had lavished upon her. He had been angry and incredulous when he realized she intended to go through with the farcical marriage.

Her brash statement that morning continued to

haunt him. "I made up my mind a long time ago that I was going to marry a rich man," Dawn had said. "The second time, I'll marry for love."

No matter how many times he told himself after that, that he was well rid of her, it never stopped him from loving her and wanting her. Dawn—with the red-gold blaze of the sun in her hair and the turquoise blue of the sea in her eyes. She was the sun and the sea to him—the heights and the depths.

Now she was coming back—a rich widow. He clamped his jaws together, wondering if she was coming back to claim the love she had discarded. At that moment, he hated her viciously. Did she think he'd still want her after all this time? Did she think she could stir up old fires and make them flame hot again? A rage seethed through him.

"How long is she staying?" Slater put his terse question to the aging guide.

"Pop never indicated that, but I got the impression he didn't expect her to come for very long—a few days maybe," he said with a vague shrug. "Course, with her money, I expect there's more exciting places to go than Key West in the summer."

"Yeah," Slater muttered a disgruntled agreement and wondered why he didn't feel more relieved.

"Look!" The urgent command from Jeeter was accompanied by a pointing finger, indicating a ten o'clock angle from the bow. "See him?"

Slater had been looking, but not seeing. "No." Then straight ahead, his eye caught the swirl of water as the wide back of a tarpon broke the surface and rolled out of sight. "There's another."

"Looks like a whole school." Jeeter leaned on the push pole to ease the skiff toward the large rolling fish. "I told you this was the place."

"You did."

With his quarry in sight, Slater made another check of his equipment to make certain the leader was knotted tightly and the line was coiled neatly where it wouldn't tangle with his feet. He waited while Jeeter poled closer, trying to concentrate on the task at hand. The fly rod was in his hand, but the excitement of pitting his skill against such a large fish with such light equipment was gone. His pleasure in the morning had faded when the conversation had turned to Dawn.

When the skiff was near enough to make a cast, Slater went through all the right motions. The colored streamer settled onto the calm surface a few inches in front of the tarpon. When the big fish struck, Slater responded automatically, pulling back three quick times to set the hook.

There was a whine of line spinning out of the reel as the tarpon took off. Leaping and twisting out of the water, it shimmered silver against the blue sky. The huge fish was easily trophy size, but there was no sense of elation in Slater. Suddenly, the line went slack, the hook thrown.

"Lost him," Jeeter announced flatly.

"It's always the big ones that get away," Slater

murmured with a degree of bitter irony in his voice.

He was unwillingly made aware of the comparison between the lost tarpon and Dawn. In both instances, they had appeared to be well and truly caught only to spit out the hook before he could reel them in. And he was the one left with a bad taste in his mouth.

Her designer blue jeans rode easily on her hips, the denim material softened and faded from many wearings. The hint of looseness about their fit suggested a weight loss that her already slim figure didn't need. Her tan boots were custom-made from hand tooled leather and the topaz blouse she wore was made from imported silk.

Devoid of any jewelry, Dawn Lord nee Canady stood at the back screen door and stared through the wire mesh at her father so earnestly engaged in a conversation with her son—his grandson—on the rear stoop. He was trying so hard to make up for lost time—for the years when Randy had been growing up without the benefit of a grandfather's company. She felt a twinge of pain—for the guilt that wouldn't let her return to the Keys, and for the pride that had kept her parents from accepting money from her to pay their way to Texas.

As her gaze lingered on Randy, there was a troubled light in the deep blue of her eyes. At ten years old, Randy was tall for his age—tall with unruly dark hair that never would behave, and gray-blue eyes that were more often confused and uncertain than happy. At the moment, they were sparkling with eagerness as Randy finally prodded her father into action.

"Mom!" He glanced toward the screen door and saw her silhouette darkening the mesh. "Gramps and I are going for a walk."

"Okay." She acknowledged the information while her thumbs remained hooked in the belt loops of her jeans, not bothering to wave a farewell as grandfather and grandson wandered out of her view.

"Gramps." Her mother's voice came from behind her, repeating the term as if the sound of it gave her pleasure. "Your father will be busting his buttons if Randy calls him that in front of his friends. He's been showing them pictures of that boy since the day Randy was born. Now, he's finally got the real thing."

"Yes," Dawn murmured, swiveling slightly to glance at her mother when she came to the screen door to stand next to her.

"To tell you the truth, I don't know which of them was more anxious to go for that walk," her mother declared with a silent laugh.

"I know what you mean." Dawn turned away from the door, but she thought she knew who would have won that contest, because she knew why Randy was so eager to explore the town. It worried her.

"There's one slice of Key lime pie left. Are you sure you don't want it?" Her mother offered for the second time. "Your father and Randy will just fight over it when they come back."

"No, honestly I don't have room for another thing," she insisted, pressing a hand against a stomach that was already filled with her mother's home-cooking. "Besides, it's fattening."

Reeta Canady skimmed her with an assessing look. "It seems to me you could stand to gain some weight."

Dawn didn't respond to that. "I'll have a cup of coffee though, if there's any left," she said instead.

"You sit at the table and I'll bring it."

A protest formed, but Dawn sensed her mother welcomed an excuse to wait on her, wanting to spoil her as she always had. Dawn didn't want to take that little pleasure from her mother. She had gone to so much trouble to fix a special lunch to welcome her home, but she still felt Dawn was accustomed to better. Better by whose standards?

Taking a seat, Dawn rested her hands on the table top. Her fingers twisted and weaved together in small movements, nervous movements that betrayed her inner agitation.

Reeta Canady was attuned to all the fine changes in her daughter since the funeral of her son-in-law. The subdued behavior, the weight loss, and the troubled distraction might all be attributable to grief, but Reeta didn't think so. With two cups of coffee poured, she set one on the table in front of Dawn. It was a bit startling to her at times that she had given birth to this stunning and vibrantly beautiful creature. Pulling up another chair, Reeta joined her at the table. There was subconscious satisfaction that she might be able to help her daughter in some way—a daughter who had everything—looks, money, and position.

"Something's bothering you. I can tell," she announced gently. "Would you like to talk about it?"

Dawn flashed her a surprised but grateful glance, then smiled ruefully. "Mother, I just got home less than two hours ago. Let's leave all the confessions until tomorrow and enjoy being together." Her problems would keep, and it wasn't fair to spoil this homecoming day for her mother.

"Where's all your jewelry?" her mother asked, sharply alert to the bareness of Dawn's fingers. "Your wedding ring? And the big solitaire?"

Dawn resisted the impulse to hide her hands in her lap and curved them around the coffee cup instead. Without the rings, her fingers felt oddly light and naked. A long sigh came from her.

"I sold them."

There was a moment of silent shock before her mother managed to ask a confused, "Why?"

The corners of her mouth bowed down in a humorless smile. "I needed the money."

"What are you talking about?" Reeta Canady showed her puzzled surprise, then didn't wait for Dawn to answer as she leaped to a conclusion. "Did Simpson lose all his money? Is that why he had his heart attack?"

"No, Mother," Dawn answered patiently. "If there was anything that caused his heart attack, it was overexertion and playing tennis in the heat of a Houston afternoon. As for his estate, I'm not sure anyone knows the exact figure but it will be in the tens of millions."

"Then, I don't understand." Her mother leaned back in her chair, fully confused. "Why did you need money?"

"It's very simple." She stared into the black coffee in her cup, sightlessly watching its shimmering surface catch the sunlight through the window. "Simpson didn't leave me any—or very little." Which was more precise.

"But—" Her mother faltered over the protest. "—you are his widow. That makes you entitled to a major share of his estate."

"Yes, I could contest the will and demand a widow's share," Dawn admitted. "But I'm not going to do that. Simpson did make a provision for me in his will to receive fifteen thousand dollars a year until Randy comes of age or I remarry. I think he was afraid I might embarrass the Lord family and wind up on the welfare rolls." It was meant as a joke but its humor was weak. In her heart, she knew that hadn't been Simpson's intention although some of his relations believed that.

"It still isn't fair," her mother protested. "You were married to him for eleven years."

"Yes. But we both know I married him because of his money. Simpson knew it, too, but it didn't matter to him as long as he was alive." Taking a sip of her coffee, Dawn felt no bitterness for his decision not to leave her more than a stipend. In a way, there was a certain justice in that. "On the whole, they were good years. Eventually I grew to care a lot about Simpson, even love him a little. I honestly tried to be a good wife to him. I owed him that."

"You were so young," her mother insisted poignantly and reached to cover Dawn's hand, squeezing it in deep affection with a mother's unwillingness to believe the worst of her child.

"That was no excuse." If she had learned anything in these last eleven years, it was the high price of selfishness. So many people had been hurt by it, including herself. "Now I have a chance to start over."

"What will you do?" Reeta asked with worried concern, wanting to help and not knowing how.

"I don't know." Giving rise to her agitation, Dawn pushed away from the table to stand. She wound her arms around herself in an unconsciously protective gesture, and wandered again to the screen door, half-turning to keep her mother within sight. "All the gifts Simpson gave me—the jewels, the furs—were mine to keep. But I certainly didn't need them anymore—or want them. So I sold them. They were worth three times the fifty thousand I got for them, but it's enough to buy a small house."

"Where?"

Her sidelong glance held her mother's for an instant then slid away. "I had planned to stay in Texas so Randy wouldn't have to change schools and leave his friends." Her expression became grim and resentful. "You remember that old saying: Nobody knows you when you're broke? When everyone found out I wasn't the rich widow, you'd be surprised how many friends I suddenly didn't have. Neither did Randy. That's really why I decided to leave Texas—because of Randy."

"What about Randy? How is he taking all this?" An anxious frown creased her forehead as Reeta Canady watched her daughter, feeling her pain and anger.

"It's difficult to say." Dawn sighed again and looked through the screen. "Randy holds so much inside that I don't really know what he's feeling. When Simpson died, he was angry at first, then hurt by his friends' rejection. I'm sure he's confused . . . and desperate."

"Didn't Simpson . . . I mean, in the will, did he—"

"No. Two years ago, Simpson set up a trust to fund Randy's college education but other than that, he left him nothing." Dawn arched her throat, fighting the tightness that gripped it, and shoved her hands deep into the hip pockets of her jeans. "I'm so glad now that Simpson insisted I had to tell Randy the truth when he was small. If I hadn't, I don't know if Randy could have handled all this—I don't know if I could have handled it. Now it's a relief that he's known for a long time that Simpson wasn't his natural father."

Dawn had to give full marks to her late husband for being so good to her son. He hadn't loved him like a father, but he had liked him and been kind to him. His belief in blood ties was too fierce for Simpson to ever consider adopting Randy. Only his flesh and blood would inherit the fortune his family had amassed.

"Does he know who his real father is?" her mother asked hesitantly.

Turning slowly, Dawn retraced her steps to the table and sank down in the chair. "Yes. He asked me, so I told him. I thought he had the right to know the name of his father." It was said flatly, all emotion pulled from her voice.

"I suppose he does." But it bothered Reeta.

"Randy hasn't actually said so, but I know he wants us to move here—to Key West. He's curious about his father. That's why he was so eager to go for a walk with Pop," Dawn explained with a vague weariness. "He's hoping he'll accidentally run into Slater—or see him—anything. He desperately wants a father. It wasn't so bad when Simpson was alive because Randy could pretend he had one. Now—?"

"Will you move here?" She had hardly dared to hope that Dawn, her only child, would consider coming back here where she could see them as often as she liked.

"That depends."

"On what?"

"Slater," Dawn replied, and combed the copper red hair behind her ears with a rake of her long fingernails.

"Are you going to tell him about Randy?" After all these years of silence, Reeta Canady couldn't help being surprised by this change in her daughter's attitude.

"He has a right to know, too," she said with a defensive air.

"You should have told him before," her mother declared in a rare admonishment.

"No!" It was a hard, swift denial that brought Dawn's head up sharply. Then just as quickly, her chin drooped in defeat. "Yes." She breathed out the admission. "I should have told him before, but I thought I knew it all then."

"Don't we all at eighteen," her mother murmured in sympathy.

"I have to tell Slater now. How he takes the news will determine whether we'll stay here or go somewhere else. I don't want Randy to know that. If Slater refused to acknowledge him even privately—and I wouldn't blame him if he did—I'd rather that Randy never learns that. I don't want him to be hurt anymore because of my stupidity." She picked up her cup but the coffee had become cold.

"When were you planning to go see him?" She pitied her daughter because she knew how awkward it was going to be.

"Not for a couple of days. I want to spend some time with you and Pop first." Just in case after she told Slater that the situation would turn too uncomfortable for her to stay. She knew how angry and bitter he had been when she'd jilted him. She couldn't even begin to guess how he'd react when he learned that she'd had his son.

Her mother fingered the handle of her coffee cup. "You do know Slater never married. Maybe . . . the two of you—"

"No, Mother." Dawn rejected that possibility as laughable. "After the way I treated him, there isn't any chance things could ever be the way they were between us. Marriage is out of the question even for Randy's sake. Slater despises me—and can't say that I blame him."

"I know he judged you harshly," her mother conceded. "But a lot of years have passed."

"Precisely." She seized on the latter statement. "People change, especially after they've been separated a long time. The intensity of feeling isn' there anymore. I know I'm not the same girl that sailed away from here on that yacht eleven years ago."

And she thanked God for that, even though she knew it was too late for her and Slater. She had lost him, and she didn't fool herself into believing she could ever win him back.

But just talking about him and the dilemma of her future provided some measure of relief. She hadn't meant to burden her mother with this discussion so early in her homecoming. Now that it was over, some of her tension had eased.

Picking up her coffee cup, she once again got to her feet. "We'd better get these lunch dishes washed before Randy and Pop come home and it' time to fix supper."

"You don't need to help," her mother protested. "Not your first day home. Sit down and have some more coffee. I'll do them."

"No, Mother," Dawn smiled and continued toward the sink full of dirty dishes. "I've got to get into practice again. After all, I'm not going t have a maid and cook to clean up after me anymore."

"It's good to have you home, Dawn," her mother declared, a little teary-eyed.

"It's good to be home," Dawn affirmed on a deep breath that was more positive in its outlook than her many sighs of troubled confusion.

Chapter Two

Cycling along the cobbled back streets of Key West, Dawn felt the clock turning back the years to the time when a bicycle had been her main means of transportation around the island. She could almost believe she was back in the past if it weren't for Randy on the bike ahead of her.

"Come on, slowpoke." He looked over his shoulder at her, smiling as he taunted her.

"Go ahead, speedy." She waved him on, knowing he was impatient with her lackadaisical pace. Randy seemed to be going through a phase where he had to race at everything. The faster the better was his motto. "I'll be the tortoise and catch up with you later when you're too pooped to pedal."

His long, sun-browned legs began pumping as hard as he could, gaining speed as Randy pulled back on the handlebars to raise the front wheel. Dawn shook her head in silent amusement, not understanding the excitement he derived from "popping a wheelie." A minute later, he was swooping around a corner and disappearing.

There was little chance of Randy becoming lost since it was an island town. Besides, the last two days he'd done so much exploring both on foot and on bicycle that he fairly well knew his way around.

Dawn had stayed close to home until this afternoon when Randy persuaded her to go biking with him. It was fun riding around her hometown, seeing the changes and the old haunts that hadn't perceptibly changed. At eighteen, Key West hadn't seemed to hold enough of anything for her—life, excitement, or the kind of future she had thought she wanted. Now, it seemed a good place to live and raise her son.

Located at the southernmost tip of the chain of Keys, its protective reefs and deep harbor had given Key West its beginnings as a pirate haven. Over the years there had been changing cultural influences until the town was a peculiar blend of New England fishing village, tourist-resort city, and a touch of elegance from its close neighbor, Cuba.

The blue sea surrounded it, and the blue sky covered it, and the sun warmed it all year round. Its near tropical climate nourished a profusion of plant life that gave the Keys a lushness and sense of mystery. There was a riot of color—the bright blossoms of bougainvillea, hibiscus, and poinciana growing rampantly.

Thick oleanders nearly hid the white picket fence from Dawn's sight. She caught the flash of white out of the corner of her eye and let the bike coast on the nearly level street while her attention strayed to identify it. The short driveway leading back to the house was nearly overgrown.

It was the old Van de Veere place. She and Katy Van de Veere had been close friends in school. Dawn remembered her mother mentioning that they had moved to the mainland a couple of years ago. It was sad to see the old house sitting vacant. She braked her bike to a halt along the side of the road for a longer look at this site from her girlhood days.

There had always seemed to be so much character and charm about the house. Even now, with its yard overgrown with shedding palm trees and choking oleanders, it appeared to steadfastly resist any attempt to suppress it. The style of the sturdy wooden house with its wide veranda was locally known as "Conch" architecture. Many places like this had been renovated into lovely homes. Dawn gazed at it wistfully, wishing she could take the house in hand and turn it into a home for herself and Randy.

There was an almost silent whish of bike wheels behind her. Dawn paid scant attention to the sound until she heard the sudden setting of brakes and tires skidding on the rough edge of the road. She turned in sharp alarm, expecting to see a bicycle spinning on its side and some child sprawled in the street. Instead, Randy came to a dramatic stop beside her, a mischievous grin on his face.

"Did I scare you?" he wanted to know, hoping

her answer would be affirmative. "I'll bet you thought I was going to run into you."

"No, but I did expect to see somebody sprawled in the street with their bike turned over," she said, giving him a reproving look from under the white sun visor cap she wore to shield her eyes from the glare of the sun.

"How come you're hanging around here?" Randy asked, rolling his bike back and forth, already anxious to be moving again.

"I was just looking at the house." Dawn bobbed her head in the direction of the structure, visible through the driveway. "One of my girlfriends used to live here. It's empty now, I guess."

"Boy, it looks like a jungle," he declared, looking at the thick undergrowth that had taken over the yard and was attacking the wide veranda. "It sure would be neat to explore the place."

No sooner was the thought voiced than Randy was riding his bike into the driveway. "Randy, that's private property," Dawn admonished. "You could be arrested for trespassing."

"Ahh, Mom," he complained. "I'm not going to vandalize anything. I just want a closer look. That's all."

A few feet inside the driveway, he stopped the bike and rested a foot on the ground for balance. Satisfied that his intentions were no more than that, Dawn followed him, curious herself to see the place up close.

"Look." Dawn pointed to the narrow slats in

the roof under the eaves. "That's 'Key West air-conditioning,' the old style. Those openings trap the cool breezes and carry them into the house."

"Really?" He eyed her skeptically, not sure she knew what she was talking about.

"Really," she confirmed, smiling but definite, and swung her gaze back to the house. Again, a wistful quality entered her deep blue eyes. "I really love that old house."

Randy was watching her closely, the gleam of an idea silvering through his eyes. "Why don't we buy the place, Mom?" he suggested and rushed on before she could answer. "You said you liked it, and we've got to live somewhere."

"Hold it, fella," she cautioned, fully aware of the desire behind all this. "I can't buy something just because I like it. There's a little matter of price and terms, and the cost of repairs. It's probably more than we can afford."

"We can do a lot of repairs ourselves," Randy insisted blithely. "Gramps would help. You should see the woodworking shop he's got in the garage. I'll bet he could fix just about anything."

"Your grandfather is a fine carpenter." It had been his craft all his life. "But there's plumbing and electrical wiring—and who knows what else."

"You're just guessing." He tried a different tactic. "You don't even know if there's anything wrong with the house at all."

"That's true." She was forced to concede the point. "But we don't have that much money to spend on a place that might cost a lot to maintain." She hated to keep harping on their suddenly limited finances, but Randy needed to learn that the purchase price of an object wasn't the only concern.

"Still, you could check and find out about it, couldn't you?" Randy countered with persuasive ease.

Dawn hesitated for a split second. There wasn't any harm in checking to find out how much was being asked for the house and learning what kind of condition it was in. There were a lot of "ifs" that had to be settled before going further than that.

"I'll see what I can find out," she promised, and signaled that they had lingered there long enough by turning her bike around in the driveway to head onto the street.

At the supper table that evening, Randy monopolized the conversation with a detailed account of their afternoon bike ride and managed to work in a subtle reminder of Dawn's promise.

"We stopped to look at this old house," he told his grandparents. "You should have seen the place. It was all overgrown with weeds and flowers. A girl you went to school with lived there, didn't she?" He pulled her into the conversation.

"It was the old Van de Veere place," Dawn explained while she ladled a spoonful of conch chowder to her soup bowl. "Do you know who owns it now?" She glanced at her mother with idle curiosity.

There was an almost stricken look on her mother's face, but her silence was covered by her husband, whose red hair had long ago turned white. "Doesn't that belong to—"

"I don't think so," Reeta Canady interrupted him quickly, throwing her husband a quelling look that was linked to the glance she darted at Randy. "I think some speculator from the mainland bought it, but I'm sure it's on the market, Dawn. You could check with one of the realtors."

"I'll do that," Dawn said, battening down the suspicions that had sprung to life at her mother's behavior.

"Are you thinking about buying the place?" inquired her father. "It's built solid as a rock."

"Yeah—" Randy rushed in with an affirmative answer.

"At the moment, it's mainly curiosity," she insisted, although the possibility hadn't lost its appeal.

It wasn't until after the meal was finished and Dawn was helping her mother clear the dishes from the table that her suspicions were confirmed. Both Randy and her father were in the garage workshop.

"Who owns the Van de Veere house?" she repeated the question she'd asked earlier.

"Slater MacBride," her mother admitted with a long look. "I nearly shoved a fritter in your father's mouth to shut him up from saying anything in front of Randy. I swear he talks and thinks afterwards."

"Why did he buy it?" Dawn wondered aloud as she absently stacked the dishes on the counter next to the sink.

"I imagine just for the investment," her mother shrugged. "He owns quite a bit of property, residential and commercial. Slater has done very well for himself. I—" She saw the pained look on Dawn's face and stopped, changing what she had started to say. "I'm sorry. But who's to say if you had married MacBride instead of Simpson, whether he would have turned out to be the same way," her mother offered in consolation.

"I know," Dawn sighed, but it was a case of knowing now what a precious gift love could be and how foolish she had been to think wealth was more valuable. For a long time, she had been reconciled to living with regret for the rest of her life, but that didn't stop it from hurting once in a while.

"After the wedding, Slater was—almost obsessed with making money," her mother explained with a kind of sadness in her voice and expression. "Every bit of money he earned or could beg, borrow, or steal he put into his deals— gambling everything on venture after venture." She shook her head, as if in reflective despair. "Eventually, I guess it became a habit." Lightly, she trailed her hand over the shimmering firelights in Dawn's hair, a gesture that reminded Dawn instantly of her childhood when her mother had stroked her hair, comforting her over some hurt. "But the money didn't make him any happier than it did you."

"It never makes anybody happy." There was a grim twist of her mouth into a rueful smile.

"Are you going to contact him about the house?"

Dawn turned on the faucets to fill the sink with water. "I don't think Randy will give me a minute's peace until I make some effort to find out about it," she declared on a humorless laugh. "And I guess it will give me a legitimate reason to call him . . . test the water before I have to plunge in."

"It would be a bit awkward to simply walk up to him and inform him about Randy," her mother agreed.

"That is an understatement." But Dawn was fully aware that she had put off contacting Slater long enough. There was no more reason to delay the moment that had to be faced. "I'll telephone him in the morning." Still, she gained herself one more night.

After reading the same paragraph twice without concentrating on what it said, Slater sighed in exasperation and started it a third time. Before he had finished the first sentence, extremely long in typical legal fashion, he was distracted by the opening of the door to his private office. Slater glanced up from the legal contract, irritated by the interruption. Nearly everything irritated him lately.

The instant he recognized his secretary, Helen Greenstone, his attention reverted to the document in his hand. Helen, a woman in her fifties, efficient, capable, new to the area, and a grandmother, walked over to his desk.

"There is fresh coffee made. Shall I bring you a cup, Mr. MacBride?" She was a stickler for formality, insisting on a show of respect for her employer who was nearly young enough to be her son.

"Yes, thank you." He glanced briefly at the correspondence she placed on his desk, letters requiring his signature. The telephone rang. The line of his mouth thinned at the second interruption. "Answer that for me."

Without a word, she reached for the telephone on his desk and punched the necessary line before picking up the receiver. "Mr. MacBride's office. May I help you please?" There was a pause for a response by the calling party. "Mr. MacBride?" She sent a questioning look at him to see if he wanted to take the call.

"Find out who it is." If it wasn't important, he didn't want to be bothered with it at the moment.

"Who's calling, please?" Helen Greenstone requested, then covered the mouthpiece with her hand to muffle her voice. "It's a Mrs. Lord."

Dawn. The identity of the caller shot through him like a lightning bolt, freezing him motionless for a split second. In the next, he wanted to grab the phone from the woman and hear Dawn's voice for himself. Anger tightened him that she could still generate that kind of reaction in him.

"Find out what she wants." Slater denied himself the sound of her voice, not totally trusting himself at that moment.

For the last four days, he'd been wondering if he'd see her or hear from her, if she'd have the nerve to contact him after all this time. Now that it had happened, he realized it had been like watching a burning fuse on a stick of dynamite and waiting for the explosion, not knowing when it would come. It finally had. Now there were the reverberations.

"What did you wish to speak to him about?" Helen asked. "Perhaps I can help you." There was another pause during which she glanced at Slater. "The Van de Veere house? Yes, it's for sale."

A shaft of anger plunged hotly through him at the thought of her calling him about a house!

"I'm certain I can arrange an appointment with Mr. MacBride to show you the house," his secretary stated and opened his appointment book, tapping a finger on the one o'clock slot to see if that met with his approval. He nodded curtly. "Mr. MacBride is free after lunch. Would one o'clock be convenient for you, Mrs. Lord—at the Van de Veere house?" She smiled at the receiver. "Thank you. Good day." She hung up the phone and jotted the meeting on his calendar for the day. "I'll bring you some coffee," she said and started to leave.

"No." It was a brisk refusal, which Slater

quickly followed with an ambiguous explanation. "I've changed my mind. I don't want any."

He focused his gaze on the legal contract he was studying as if it had all his attention. When the door closed behind his secretary, it strayed to the name written on the sheet in his appointment book. Slater stared at it for a long time.

Dawn was slow to replace the telephone receiver on its cradle. Her nerves were so raw she wanted to scream and release some of the tension that was building up inside her. There was a keen sense of hurt, too, because she hadn't expected to be fobbed off onto his secretary. Once she'd identified herself, she had thought she'd be put right through to Slater. Instead, she'd been forced to carry through the charade of looking at the house.

"Who were you talking to just now, Mom?"

Startled, Dawn swung around to stare at her son. She thought he was outside. Had he been listening? Was it merely the gleam of curiosity in his eyes, or the sharpness of foreknowledge? She reached out to smooth the cowlick on his forehead.

"I was making an appointment to see the man about the house you and I looked at yesterday," she admitted, smiling stiffly and excluding the information that the man was his father. A change of subject was needed. "It won't be long and you'll be as tall as I am."

"My dad is tall, isn't he?" The quietly asked question nearly undermined her.

"Yes," Dawn replied with an attempt at smoothness that didn't completely succeed. "Six foot. So you have a few more inches to grow yet."

"When are you going to talk to him about the house?" This time he changed the subject. Or so Dawn hoped.

"One o'clock this afternoon."

"Can I come with you?" he asked.

"No." She smiled to make her refusal seem less important than it was.

There was a flicker of disappointment, but it was soon replaced by a resigned acceptance. "I might go looking around the shops in Old Town after lunch. Is that all right?"

"Sure." Her smile widened with his failure to pursue coming with her.

At lunch, Dawn was too nervous to eat, her stomach churning in anticipation of the meeting with Slater. Pleading a lack of appetite she excused herself from the table and went to her old room to get ready.

It wasn't easy choosing what to wear. The near-tropical summer climate dictated light-weight clothing, but there was still the choice of casual, sporty, sophisticated. Thanks to Simpson's generosity during their marriage, Dawn had an abundant wardrobe to choose from.

After several false starts, she settled on a seersucker suit, white with thin blue stripes, and a plain silk blouse in sapphire blue. Her sandaled heels and purse were a matching shade of blue to complete the ensemble. Luckily Dawn had kept

he good pieces of costume jewelry, selling only
he gold and the jewels, so she slipped a couple of
rings on her fingers and a pair of earrings.

The mirror said the finished product looked
subtly elegant and slightly businesslike. The
curling thickness of her rich auburn tresses lay
casually about her shoulders to soften the effect.
Her expression looked a little tense, a tautness to
her mouth, but it was to be expected under the
circumstances.

When she left the house, she waved at her
mother who anxiously wished her good luck. The
moral support was gratefully received. There
was no sign of Randy as she reversed her car out
of the driveway, so she wasn't forced to tell him
again that she didn't want his company.

If it hadn't been for the afternoon heat, the
distance to the Van de Veere house could easily
have been walked, but Dawn didn't want to spoil
the freshness of her appearance. The dashboard
clock in her car, another gift from Simpson his
estate hadn't been able to claim, showed two
minutes before the hour when she turned into
the driveway.

There was no other vehicle parked there, and
no sign that anyone was around—or had been
around. As she climbed out of the car, her nerves
were jumping and her breath was running shallow and fast. The sidewalk to the front door was
nearly impassable. Dawn had to lift encroaching
branches and vines aside to reach the steps.

A breeze stirred the palm, the spiked fronds

rustling together. There was a reassuring solidness to the veranda floor as she crossed it to try the front door. It was locked, eliminating the possibility that Slater was inside waiting for her. Dawn turned, looking back to the driveway and suddenly wondering if he would come at all. Or would he thwart her by sending someone else to show her the house? A quiver of unease went through her.

From the street, there was a loud purr of a powerful car engine approaching the house. When a low, sleek Corvette turned into the driveway, a tingle of mixed relief trailed over her nerves. It stopped behind her car and the motor was killed. The minute the driver stepped out Dawn no longer had to wonder whether Slater would come himself. He was here.

Long and lean, his familiar body had retained that easy flow of movement that came with being in prime physical condition. His profile was strongly cut and sun-bronzed, and his gilded brown hair was slightly rumpled by a playing wind. A pair of sunglasses hid his eyes, but she knew he'd seen her standing on the wide veranda.

There was an instant's pause before he removed them and tossed them through the opened car window onto the seat. Without another glance in her direction, Slater wound his way through the tangle of underbrush encroaching on the path to the steps.

In those first seconds, she was struck by all the

40

things that were familiar about him. But as he came closer, she became aware of the changes. No more faded jeans, worn soft to hug his thighs, no more T-shirts stretched thin to mold his flatly muscled chest and shoulders, no more soiled sneakers without socks on his feet.

The way he was dressed was a stark contrast to the past. From the fine leather of his polished shoes to the continental cut of his brown slacks and the print silk shirt tapered to fit, Slater MacBride was the model of what the successful man looked like . . . casual—the shirt unbuttoned at the throat—and confident.

The softness of youth was gone from his features, that love of a good time which had once creased it with eagerness. Maturity had brought a hard definition to the male angles of his face, adding more emphasis to virility than to mere handsomeness.

But all the changes were unquestionably improvements. All her senses, everything inside her seemed to rush out, reaching for him. It was like a torrent being unleashed, a torrent of love and regret that seemed to spill from her in waves, yet she never moved, never took a step forward to greet him, and never changed her expression. The tumultuous reaction was all contained inside. Dawn had learned too well, during her marriage to Simpson, how to hide her true feelings.

When she finally met the flint-gray in his eyes, she was glad she hadn't begun the meeting on an emotional note. The aloofness in his gaze was chilling. When she finally spoke, she felt she was literally breaking the ice.

"Hello, Slater." Her voice was smooth and even. "It's good to see you looking so well."

"Thank you." He inclined his head at the compliment with a thick trace of mockery. "Or, perhaps I should say 'thanks to you.'" The barbed correction was accompanied by a challenging flick of his brow, but he continued smoothly without waiting for a response. "I'd like to take the opportunity to offer you my condolences on the untimely death of your husband."

She doubted it was a sincere offer of sympathy, but she didn't question it. "Thank you," she murmured.

His gaze made a sweep of her. "I expected to find you elegantly clad in black, Mrs. Lord—the grieving widow mourning for her beloved husband." There was a mocking twist of his mouth. "But these days, I guess not even the rich follow the custom of wearing black."

"That's true," she admitted, refusing to take offense at his thinly veiled jibes. She had not arranged to meet him to take part in a war of words, with herself constantly on the defensive, so she was determined not to parry any of his sharp thrusts. "It's no longer considered improper to wear other colors."

"Pity. You would be stunning in black," he murmured with a lazy glance at her fiery mane of hair, but his coolness took any hint of a compliment from his voice.

Dawn was stiff, trying to keep in check the natural instinct to defend herself from his subtle attack. "I'll try to remember that," was the most indifferent reply she could make, but even it betrayed that his stinging comments were getting through.

"You have a slight accent," Slater observed.

"Have I?"

"After living so long in Texas, I guess it's to be expected," he said with an uncaring shrug, then smiled. "But you don't need to be concerned. A little drawl is very sexy, but then—it goes with the body, doesn't it?"

Despite the rake of his eyes, Dawn had the feeling Slater didn't find her at all sexually appealing. It seemed he had crushed out every feeling for her. Had she really thought it would be otherwise? She dug her long nails into her palm, resisting the impulse to slap him and hurt him physically the way he was hurting her mentally. Any other response was impossible so she made none.

Her silence seemed to irritate him, however briefly. "I believe you were interested in this house." He reached in his pocket for the key and moved past her to unlock the front door. "I only acquired the property recently so I haven't had the opportunity to have the yard cleaned up and the house put in order. Naturally the price will be reduced to compensate for its neglected condition." Pausing, he pushed the door open and turned to hold her gaze. "That is, if you are actually interested in purchasing it?"

43

It was the skepticism in his eyes that prompted Dawn to put him through the formality of showing her the house, although she had serious doubts that a sale would ever come to pass. For a moment she wanted to forget about her true purpose in meeting him and avoid all this unpleasantness. But she recognized it was a selfishly motivated desire. There was Randy's need to consider as well.

"I am interested," she stated and walked past him to enter the house, stale and musty from being shut up for so long—like their relationship. Perhaps an airing was all that was needed for them, too. Dawn suspected that was purely wishful thinking.

Chapter Three

Dust had naturally accumulated on the window-sills and floors. A cupboard door or two in the kitchen had swelled shut, but there were no major things wrong. None of the ceilings showed any signs of roof leakage. There weren't any rust stains from leaky water pipes. Without furniture in the rooms or curtains at the windows, the house had a starkness to it, but now and then Dawn caught traces of the character she remembered as Slater toured her through the rooms.

Coming full circle back to the living room, Slater paused inside the arched doorway. Behind his lazy regard of her, there was an intensity that had persisted each time he looked at her. It made Dawn uncomfortable and tense, as if she never dared to relax. She made a show of ignoring him, her glance wandering around the room instead.

"Trying to decide which wall to hang your Picasso on?" Slater queried mockingly. "It might look out of place in these simple surroundings."

"Why should it?" She swung around to face him, half the width of the empty room separating them. "The ceramic cat Picasso designed for

Hemingway is displayed in the house where he lived here in Key West." She was tired of his constant jibes about money and cultural status. "There's a whole colony of artists and craftsmen here."

"But not jetsetters, or the wealthy elite," Slater countered. There was a lazy curve to his mouth, but it held more mockery than amusement. "Their gathering place is Key Largo. Maybe that's why I have trouble believing you are actually serious about buying this house. Or are you trying to make this area the new 'in' place for rich snowbirds?" His taunting voice continued to challenge her. "How much time will you spend here? A week a year? Two weeks?"

"Key West is my hometown," Dawn reminded him. "Why is it so impossible to think that I might want to live here?"

"Maybe because you've stayed away for ten years."

"Eleven," she corrected.

A shoulder lifted in an uncaring shrug. "Who's counting?" It was obvious he wasn't. That hurt almost more than anything else he'd said.

"You're right." Her voice went flat.

"Why did you really want to see this house, Mrs. Lord?" he challenged.

He deliberately kept using her married name, constantly reminding Dawn of her perfidy. She wanted to scream at him to stop it, the sound of it scraping over her raw nerves, but she didn't.

"I've already told you," she insisted stiffly.

"It's a lovely old home," Slater said idly. "A

46

bargain. I guess that's the problem. I don't see you as a bargain-hunter—" There was an abrupt pause. "I guess you are at that. You like to look over the merchandise and shop for the best deals, don't you?"

"What am I supposed to say to that?" she demanded, bristling at his constant harangue.

"If the shoe fits?" he murmured and left the rest of the old saying unfinished.

"Sometimes people outgrow old shoes." It was the closest she'd come to denying his veiled accusations against her character.

Now that she had finally risen to his baiting remarks Slater seemed to tire of the sport. "About this house—" he began. "You have seen the condition it's in. If you're serious about buying, we'll get down to the business of price and terms. Even if you don't choose to live in it, the property would be a sound investment."

"I'm considering possibly moving here permanently," Dawn stated, drawing his sharpened glance.

"Depending on what?" Slater sensed the unspoken qualification in her announcement.

"Depending on you." The conversation had finally come around to the subject she needed to discuss with him, and she drew her first calm breath, the moment finally coming.

But the calm didn't last more than a second. The stale air became suddenly charged with a volatile energy. Slater discarded his pose of lazy mockery as his features hardened in contemptuous anger and his gray eyes smouldered.

"That's rich!" He breathed out the harsh words, his jaw rigidly clenched. "You don't give a damn about me! You don't care about anybody but yourself and what you want!"

Her gaze faltered under the censorious glare of his. She tightened her grip on the blue purse, glancing at her whitened knuckles briefly.

"I don't blame you for thinking that way about me. Heaven knows I've given you cause," Dawn admitted, managing to keep her voice even. "What I did was wrong. I know that now. And I'm sorry."

"And what does that mean?" He moved toward her, one slow step gliding into the next.

It wasn't until he stopped inches in front of her that Dawn realized how much he had kept his distance from her. Now he was all too close, so tall, wider in the shoulders than she remembered. She felt the rush of adrenaline through her veins, heightening all her senses.

"It means I'm truly sorry I hurt you." There was no adequate elaboration she could make on the apology to convince him she was sincere.

His mouth was pulled straight in a hard line, a muscle jumping on the high ridge of his jaw. "I'm sorry I hurt you," Slater repeated her words in a tautly flat voice. "As if I'd been knocked down and skinned my knee." He dismissed the apology as small compensation for the pain she had caused him. "I loved you." The declaration was pushed through his teeth, fierce and low. "When you married him, you took everything—my heart, my pride, my all. You left me barren and empty—like this house! Crying out for—for you!"

The sting of tears was in her eyes, sharp remorse twisting like a knife in her heart. Dawn met the harshness of his gaze without blinking. At the time, she had been too selfish to see the full consequences of her action, the ripple effect her decision had made, first striking Slater, then Simpson, Randy, even her parents.

"I know," she said. "I had hoped time would have healed some of the pain." Or at least tempered some of his anger, but it hadn't.

"Why?" Slater demanded. "Did you think you could come back and pick up where we left off? Did you think you could kiss away the hurt that was left and make it better?" His hands gripped her arms, his fingers digging into the seersucker sleeves of her light jacket. "Why don't you see if it works?"

The snarling challenge was no sooner issued than Slater was pulling her roughly against him to have it carried through. An arm was hooked behind her waist while eleven years of bitterness, anger, and loathing came crushing down on her mouth. Dawn was rigid against this punishing sexual assault, powerless but unyielding.

The hardness of his mouth ground her lips against her teeth, not taking any effort to make the bruising kiss anything but unpleasant. The humiliating sensation was so at odds with the stimulating scent of spicy male cologne that assailed her nose, and with the evocative familiarity of his lean, muscled body molded so tightly to hers.

There was only one purpose to this embrace—to hurt and degrade her mentally and physically the way she had injured him. And Slater was resorting to the base tactic of sexual force to accomplish it. Even while Dawn hated him for treating her so brutally, she couldn't cast stones with a free conscience.

The grinding pressure of his mouth gradually eased as he slowly broke the contact. Dawn remained motionless, a prisoner in his arms. Her eyes closed as she tried to piece together her pride. His fanning breath was warm and moist against her sore lips, his breathing labored and uneven.

"Damn you." There was frustration in the hoarseness of his low curse as if the result of his abusiv~ kiss hadn't been as satisfying as he had expected it to be.

Slowly Dawn raised her lashes to look at him. He was so close she could count the number of tiny white suncreases around his half-closed eyes. Mixed in with the bitter pain, she could see the want that was darkening his gray eyes. Her breath caught in her throat.

His hand moved slowly along her spine, no longer imprisoning but exploring instead with almost reluctant interest. She was conscious of the feel of his body shaped so fully to hers and the ache of desire in his eyes. Memories came rushing back of a time when his touch had excited her beyond all measure, making it easy to forget something so unpleasant as the events of a minute ago. The protective tension faded, taking the stiffness from her limbs, letting her go soft against him.

"Why did you have to come back?" he groaned in a kind of despair. "I was just getting to the point where I could hear your name without going to pieces."

"I was such a fool, Slater." Caught in the emotional moment, Dawn nearly sobbed out the admission.

When her arms went around his neck to make her a participant instead of a victim of his embrace, it was only instinct that prompted her fingers to retain their grip on her clutch purse. This time eleven years of hunger were unleashed when his mouth moved onto her swollen lips. The rawness of his need evoked a tumultuous response that sent her heart soaring.

She strained to fulfill it, wanting to give back more than she got. She was the aggressor. Her fingers curled into the virile thickness of his hair, forcing his head to increase its angle and the pressure of his kiss, while the driving probe of her tongue pushed its way between his lips to intimately deepen the kiss. She could feel the hammering of his heart, only a beat behind the racing tempo of her own.

His hands were caressing, roaming at will over her back and shoulders and stirring up passions that had lain dormant for so long. It was not that Simpson had been sexually unsatisfying as a lover, but there had not been this volatility that was created by the combination of physical and emotional desire. Time hadn't altered this feeling they shared. Dawn recognized that, and there was a wild singing in her veins at the discovery that she found what she thought had been irrevocably lost.

Abruptly, almost violently, Slater was pulling her arms from around his neck and pushing her from him. Dawn was stunned by the fury she saw in his expression. Cold and bitter rejection was taking the place of the desire that had glittered in his eyes.

"Your husband has only been in the ground a month and already you're trying to seduce another man into your bed," accused Slater. "But you're not going to sucker me a second time, *Mrs. Lord.*"

"No. Slater—" She was wounded by his sarcasm, which was for once totally unjustified. Regardless of what he thought, that hadn't been her intention in meeting him.

"You warned me eleven years ago." There was disgust in his sweeping visual assessment of her. "But I didn't think even you would have the gall to do it. 'The second time for love,' isn't that what you said? But first you were going to marry money." His mouth curled with contempt.

"Don't." It was a quiet protest, because there was no point in going into all that.

But Slater took no notice of it. "Well, you've got your money now, don't you?" he taunted. "The Widow Lord and all her Texas millions."

Dawn didn't correct his impression that Simpson had bequeathed her the bulk of his estate. Her wealth, or lack of it, wasn't the issue that had brought her here, so she didn't want the distraction of discussing it. Besides, it wasn't any of Slater's business.

"You came back to see if that love you threw away eleven years ago was still around. Did you really think I'd want you?" There was a rigid movement of his head, a kind of negative shake that was heavy with disdain. "You can take your money and your love—and you know what you can do with it!"

Dawn spoke quickly when he started to swing away to leave. "That isn't why I came back, Slater."

"Isn't it?" His mouth was slanted in a cruelly mocking line.

"There are a lot of reasons why I haven't been back before now, but there is only one reason why I wanted to see you privately today," she stated, a steadiness finally returning to her voice after the passionately disturbing kiss. "When I told you that I hoped you wouldn't be so bitter after this much time, it was the truth. Not because I wanted to pick up where we left off. I don't expect us to be lovers. I doubt if we can even be friends."

"I'm glad you see that so clearly, because you destroyed any future for us eleven years ago," he returned grimly. "Don't forget to shut the door when you leave."

"Wait." Her voice checked the stride he had

taken toward the door. Impatience vibrated in his glance as Slater half-turned. "There's something I have to tell you."

"I can't think of anything you have to tell me that I would be interested to hear," he stated flatly, and started again for the door.

"Not even about your son?" Dawn asked and watched him freeze, then slowly turn to face her.

His probing gaze was hard with anger. "What is that supposed to mean?" he demanded with an openly skeptical expression.

"I'm talking about Randy—my son. *Our* son." Her voice remained level, containing a degree of false calm under his narrowing gaze. "You are his father."

The silence lengthened into interminable seconds without his expression changing from its hard and doubting contempt. "You haven't changed a bit." His low pronouncement reached out to strike her down. "You'll use any trick in the book to get what you want. Even to the extent of trying to tie me to you by pretending I fathered your son." He shook his head, suddenly becoming totally indifferent. "It won't work."

"Randy is your son," Dawn insisted, but Slater was already striding to the door. She started after him. "If you'd just let me explain—"

The door was pulled shut behind his retreating figure, ending her sentence before it was finished. Dawn stopped and stared at the door, stunned by his reaction to the news. She had prepared herself mentally for bitterness, anger, and outrage—even doubt—but she hadn't expected Slater to dismiss t as an impossibility and refuse to listen to what she had to say.

A despairing depression settled heavily onto her shoulders. Dawn turned, her gaze running sightlessly around the empty room. Dust particles danced in the sunlight streaming through a window. What proof could she show Slater that he would believe? If he refused to hear her out, what could she do?

Outside, a car engine growled to life and accelerated, its transmission being shifted into reverse gear. There was something final about the fading sound of Slater's driving away. Unsure what her next move would be, Dawn walked to the door through which Slater had so recently exited the house. The self-locking latch clicked as she closed it and crossed the veranda.

Her thoughts were as crowded and tangled as the lush, green foliage pressing in on all sides. No solution worked its way through her troubled confusion to show her a clear path. Dawn followed the weed-riddled sidewalk to the driveway and her parked car.

Reeta Canady heard the car turn into the driveway and was out the back door before Dawn could slide from behind the wheel. She knew her daughter's decision to live permanently in Key West was riding on the outcome of this meeting with Slater MacBride. And she was anxious to know the result, wanting her daughter and grandchild to stay and crossing her fingers that it would come to pass.

"What happened?" Her searching gaze made a hurried inspection of her daughter's troubled countenance as she tried to guess what it meant.

"Where's Randy?" Dawn asked, glancing around for her son. This was one conversation she didn't want him to accidentally overhear. Until she had decided how to handle this situation, she didn't want Randy to know anything about her meeting with his natural father.

"I saw him ride by on his bike about an hour ago with two other boys his age. I knew it wouldn't be long before he made some friends here," her mother replied, anxious to assert something positive into the negative atmosphere she felt. "I don't expect he'll be back until supper time."

His usual parking stall was unoccupied when Slater returned to the building in Old Town that housed his office. The area was cluttered with tourists, young and old alike. Slater was too preoccupied to take notice of any of them, his expression grim and haunted as he rode the brake and swung the low-slung sportscar into its stall.

With a turn of the key, he switched off the powerful engine. Its demise finally brought an end to the invisible fire that had been burning at his heels, driving him out of the house and away from Dawn. If he had stayed any longer, she would have gotten to him again.

From the moment he'd set eyes on her when he stepped out of the car, the same old excitement had started rising in him. He'd known that he didn't dare get near enough to touch her. But the temptation had been stronger than his willpower could resist.

It had been curiosity that had prompted him to keep the appointment, a desire to prove that he no longer wanted her. But it had backfired in his face. The long abstinence had not eased his craving for her. Like an alcoholic who didn't dare take another sip, he should never have taken that first kiss. He was hooked all over again. Slater hated himself for that, and he hated her, too, in that strange way when a man loves too deeply.

Impatience and frustration marked his movements as Slater stepped crisply out of the car. His coiled muscles rippled with the containment of volatile energy in his whipped-lean body. He started toward his office.

A young boy had stopped his bike behind the black sportscar and appeared to be admiring its sleek lines. He smiled quickly at Slater when he drew nearer. "Hi." It was a bright greeting, issued with guilty swiftness as if the boy was being caught doing something he shouldn't.

Slater nodded to him curtly, not in the mood to converse with some juvenile. But the bold youth didn't take the hint.

"Is this your car?" he asked, setting the kickstand so the bike stood upright on its own.

Slater's first impulse was to ignore the question and keep walking. But he was slowed by a twinge of guilt at the unfairness of taking out his bad temper by being rude to the boy.

"Yes, it is." Politeness put little warmth in his voice, but he did respond.

His gaze made a flicking, uninterested study of the boy, a gangly mixture of arms and legs with dark, russet-brown hair and light blue eyes. Although the bike was dented and rusted in spots, it was obviously rented, because the boy was dressed in expensive clothes, exclusive labels plainly displayed on the knit shirt and designer denim jeans. The youth was obviously the son of some wealthy tourist. It was an observance Slater made without caring much about the conclusion he had reached. Taking note of such details had become second nature to him.

"Boy, it's really something," the lad exclaimed. "How fast will it go?"

This fascination with speed brought a brief twitch of amusement to Slater's mouth. It was typical of the young, the demand for action and excitement.

"Fast enough," he returned, aware the boy's glance was continually darting to him. Something wasn't quite right here. Although the boy was expressing interest in the sportscar, he seemed more intent on studying him. Slater observed a hint of strain and tension in the boy's features. Did it come from excitement or the manifestation of nervousness?

"I'd sure like to have a car like this when I'm older," the boy said in a voice that held a poignant ring of longing.

Bothered by something he couldn't identify, Slater narrowed his study of the boy. Before he could reply, he was hailed by a voice coming from up the street.

"Hey, MacBride!"

He turned to observe the approach of his long-time friend and local fishing guide, Jeeter Jones. With the spry, rolling step of a seaman, Jeeter closed the distance between them. His leathered face was cracked by a greeting smile.

"How are you doing, Jeeter?" Slater felt a surge of impatience at this second delay and wished he had not stopped to speak to this boy. It wasn't company he wanted. It was privacy to deal with the emotions meeting Dawn again had aroused.

"Thought I'd come by and see if I couldn't talk you into buying me a cup of coffee," Jeeter explained and glanced curiously at the boy, who was taking advantage of Slater's distraction to stare raptly at him. "Who's your young friend?" Something about the boy struck a familiar chord and Jeeter darted a quick look at Slater and found it repeated.

With the arrival of Jeeter Jones, Slater had forgotten about that earlier moment when something about the boy had bothered him. His mildly indifferent glance slid to the youth.

"He was admiring my car," Slater explained, then addressed the boy, remembering his previous comment about owning a car like it someday. "Maybe your father will buy you one when you're older." Judging from the way the boy was dressed, his parents could afford it.

There was a sudden flood of red into the boy's cheeks. "Yeah," he mumbled the answer and turned quickly to his bike, hiding the betraying surge of embarrassment. Kicking the stand back, he hopped onto the seat and pedaled away.

The abruptness of his departure pulled Slater's gaze after him. The boy didn't travel far, stopping at the first street vendor he reached. As he looked over the assortment of cookies and cold drinks, the boy stole a glance over his shoulder at Slater and quickly averted his gaze when he saw Slater watching him.

A snorting sound, like a contained laugh, came from Jeeter Jones. "I knew you'd sown some wild seeds in your time, MacBride, but I didn't expect to see the crop maturing so close to home."

Slater swung his gaze around to subject Jeeter to his piercing scrutiny. "What are you talking about?"

"That boy," Jeeter said. "He's darn near the spittin' image of you right down to the cowlicks in his hair. What is he? Some cousin of yours?"

Too stunned to reply, Slater stared at his friend for a blank second. Then his head jerked around to stare at the boy still hovering about the vendor's cart. It wasn't possible! Dawn had been lying. He would have bet his life on it. But—he had to find out. Whipping off his dark glasses, he jammed them into his shirt pocket so they wouldn't shade something from his sight and prevent him from seeing something he should.

Turning away from Jeeter, he broke into a jog. "Hey! What about the coffee?" Jeeter protested in a startled voice.

"Another time." The answer was thrown over his shoulder, his gaze not straying from the boy, who noticed his approach and appeared to tense up. Slater lengthened his stride and weaved through the few pedestrians in his path.

There was a pallor beneath the boy's tanned face as he hurriedly dug into the pocket of his jeans to pay for the limeade he'd ordered. He was still trying to count out the money when Slater arrived at the cart.

Taking two dollar bills from his pocket, Slater laid them atop the cart. "I'll buy his, Rufus," he told the man. "Give me a limeade, too."

After an interested glance that took in both Slater and the boy, the vendor gave a small shrug and turned to fill a plastic glass with the chilled, fresh-squeezed juice.

"I've got the money to pay for my own, sir," the boy declared, suddenly very stiff and warily nervous with Slater there.

"I know." His eyes were taking in the youth-softened yet strongly chiseled lines of the boy's features, the trace of blue in his gray eyes, and the mop of dark hair that rebelled against any orderly style. "What's your name?" He picked up the two glasses, but withheld giving one to the boy.

"Randy," he mumbled, trying but not quite meeting Slater's look.

"Your full name," Slater prompted and offered one of the glasses.

There was a moment of indecision before the

boy answered. "Randy MacBride Lord." Then he looked up to watch Slater's reaction, wary and defensive.

The answer confirmed what Slater had doubted all along. The sudden burden of it removed all emotion from him, wiping him clean like a blackboard.

"Do you know who I am?" he asked with a lack of expression that bordered on a deceptive nonchalance.

Again, he was subjected to a measuring study by the boy before Randy affirmed his knowledge with a slow nod of his head. It was followed by an equally hesitant—"You're Slater MacBride"—as if Randy didn't want to admit how much he knew.

"I met your mother today," Slater said.

"I know," Randy said, then explained, "I saw your car parked in the driveway behind hers when I rode by the house on my bike. Did she—" he faltered, lowering his gaze to nervously study the handlebars of his bike, "—did she . . . tell you about me?"

"Yes." Slater released a bitter, laughing breath that held no humor. "It seems I'm the last one to know." He noticed the moisture gathering in Randy's eyes and his desperate attempt to hide the tears. It tugged at something in his heart. A new gentleness entered his voice when Slater spoke again. "I think it's time you and I talked about a few things."

"Yes, sir." There was a hopeful tremor in Randy's voice.

"Why don't you lock up your bike in that rackstand over there?" Slater nodded to one positioned at the corner. "Then we'll go walk somewhere and find a place to drink our limeade."

"Okay." Randy pushed his bike toward the stand with a betraying eagerness.

Chapter Four

Her shoulder-length red hair was tied atop her head in a short ponytail to keep the hot weight of it off her neck while she helped her mother fix the evening meal. Dawn dabbed at the perspiration beading in the hollow of her throat from the heat of the stove. She poked a fork into the potatoes to test whether they were done. It broke into pieces at the touch of the fork tines. She turned off the burner beneath the pan.

"The potatoes are almost mush," she announced to her mother and turned. "Any sign of Randy yet?"

Her mother peered out the window above the sink where she was tearing lettuce leaves to make a salad. "I don't see him. Maybe he's in the garage with your father."

"I'll see." Dawn moved away from the stove and walked to the screen door.

Outside, she made a quick scan of the backyard, looking for Randy's bike. There were hammering sounds coming from the garage and Dawn headed toward the raised door. The garage was so crowded with pieces of wood, slabs of cypress trunks, and objects in various stages of completion that there wasn't any room for a car.

Without attempting to work her way through the obstacle course of nails, sawdust, and the lumber-strewn floor, Dawn paused inside the opening and called to her father, raising her voice to make herself heard above the racket of his hammering. "Hey, Pop!"

He straightened from his workbench and turned, taking a mouthful of nails from his mouth. "Time for supper?" he guessed.

"Yes. But I'm looking for Randy. Has he come home yet?" she frowned.

"Haven't seen him all afternoon," he said with a shake of his head, then laid his tools on the counter and turned to walk through the maze on a path only he could discern. "I'm going to get all this cleaned up someday. Problem is, I've run out of friends to give all this stuff to."

Dawn glanced at the cypress clock propped against a wall and a uniquely styled chair with a cypress slab seat, two of the rare pieces that were finished and now gathering dust. "Instead of giving them away, you should sell them," she advised. The garage contained everything from handmade furniture to lamps to polished pieces of driftwood and sculptures made out of shells and carved wood.

"It wouldn't be fair." He shrugged aside the craftsmanship of the products. "It's just something I do to pass the time."

"Puttering or not, it's better than some of the stuff I've seen in the shops," Dawn declared, then turned her gaze toward the driveway. "I wonder where Randy is."

Her father laid a hand on her shoulder in an affectionate gesture that also pushed her toward the house. "He'll be here directly. He probably just lost track of the time. But don't worry, that bottomless stomach of his will soon be reminding him it's supper time."

Dawn let herself be guided to the house, but she was still bothered by Randy's absence.

A quarter of an hour later, all the food was ready to be dished up and served. Her father had returned to the kitchen from washing his hands and took his customary chair at the head of the table. Dawn was growing impatient and irritated at her son's tardiness.

"Isn't Randy here yet?" her father asked.

"No." Her hands were on her hips, betraying the suppressed anger with her stance, as she looked out the rear screen door for the umpteenth time.

"It's all right," her mother insisted. "We can keep the food hot a while longer."

"It is not all right, Mother," Dawn retorted. "Randy knows what time we have supper. It's rude and thoughtless of him to keep us waiting."

"I'm sure he's probably having such a good time playing with his new friends that he just hasn't realized how late it is." Her mother provided an excuse for the absent Randy. "It isn't like him to deliberately stay gone without reason."

Once Dawn would have agreed with that, because Randy had always been well-mannered and considerate of others. But, since Simpson had died, there had been a couple of isolated incidents when Randy had been deliberately uncaring of the inconvenience he had caused others. She didn't know whether it was a phase he was going through or if he was testing her authority now that Simpson wasn't around to enforce the rules.

"We've already waited supper almost an hour for him," Dawn reminded her mother. "It will be ruined if you try to keep it hot any longer. You two go ahead and eat. I'm going out to look for Randy."

"There's no need for that," her father inserted. "Sooner or later, he's going to come home. When he does, he'll have to eat a cold supper. That will be a good lesson for a boy with Randy's appetite."

But if it was discipline he was unconsciously seeking by staying away—proof that Dawn cared enough for him—then the passive punishment of a cold supper would not accomplish anything. She couldn't begin to guess the motive behind his absence, if there was one, but she intended to find out.

"Maybe so, but I'm going out to look for him just the same," she stated.

"Aren't you going to have supper with us first?" her mother protested as Dawn started out the door.

"No," she paused long enough to answer. "And

don't bother to save anything for Randy and me. I'll fix us something to eat when we come back."

The three most logical places where Randy might be tarrying were the beach, the marina, or the area of Old Town. All of them were within walking distance, but Dawn decided she could cover the areas more quickly by car.

The first two were easy. She drove slowly past the public beach areas. Most of the bathers had forsaken the sand now that the sun was hanging low in the sky and the dinner hour had arrived. The same was true at the marina. The fishermen had already come in with their day's catches and dispersed. Dawn didn't find Randy among the few people still lingering in the two areas.

Old Town proved to be too congested with foot and wheel traffic. The sidewalk restaurants were crowded with customers combining the outdoor dining experience with people-watching. There were too many directions to look at the same time and still keep her attention on the road.

Giving up, Dawn parked the car and continued her search on foot. The more she looked, the more irritated she became. Always the thought was at the back of her mind that Randy might already be home while she was out here walking the streets looking for him. It didn't improve her temper.

Intent on some boys Randy's age engaged in horseplay across the street, Dawn didn't see the tropically dressed pair of tourists until she had bumped into the man. At the last second, she tried to avoid the collision by stepping sideways, but she careened off the bikestand right into the man.

The impact staggered her. She stepped all over the man's toes as she attempted to regain her balance. Finally his steadying hands managed to right her and get her sandaled feet off his toes.

"I'm sorry," Dawn apologized profusely to the middle-aged man. "I'm afraid I wasn't watching where I was going."

"No harm done," he insisted with only a trace of a wince from the injury to his exposed toes in the leather beach thongs. The lovely sight before him seemed ample compensation for any harm she had done to him. His onlooking wife was forgotten as the male tourist got an eyeful of Dawn in her white shorts and clinging knit tank-top.

"Come on, Herb," his wife snapped in irritation at the way he was ogling Dawn.

With a shrugging smile of regret, he stepped to the side to let Dawn pass by, stealing a glance at her rear view before his wife tugged him forward.

Her shin throbbed from its collision with the bikestand. Dawn paused to rub it and glance at the guilty object that had bruised it. Her gaze fastened on the old bike parked in the rack. It looked just like the one Randy had been using. Surely no two bikes would have matching dents and that funny rust pattern on the front fender. A

closer look at the lock securing it to the stan
confirmed that it was Randy's. Her father's ini
tials were engraved into the base.

She straightened, looking intently up an
down the street. Randy was around here some
where, and not on his way home. But where
She'd looked in nearly every shop and walked a
the streets.

Dawn had barely asked herself the questio
when she came up with the answer. "Mallor
Pier, of course," she murmured.

It had become the evening gathering place an
center of activity until the sun went down. Sh
struck out for the pier, certain now that sh
would find Randy there.

When she reached it, the pier was alread
crowded with people. There was an almost fest
val atmosphere about the place. Everyone cam
to watch the sun make its daily spectacula
descent into the Gulf of Mexico. It was an idea
setting with a backdrop of all water and sky.

The mood of the revelers didn't touch Dawr
too intent on finding her errant son to care abou
the party atmosphere. All sorts of amateur er
tertainers were displaying their talents to th
assembled crowd. Passing a juggler, Dawn cor
tinued looking into faces. There were so man
young people around that their features seeme
to blur together, making her wonder if she'd b
able to recognize Randy in this sea of teenager
and pre-teens.

Her patience had nearly worn thin when sh
finally saw him. He was standing at the end of

group, munching on a conch fritter and laughing at the antics of a mime. Randy said something to the man beside him, drawing the sparkling impatience of her gaze to him.

The anger drained from her with a rush as she recognized Slater. For an instant, he was all she could see. As if sensing he was being watched, his gaze suddenly scanned the crowd around him and came to a stop on her. She could almost feel the boring thrust of his gaze impaling her.

A thousand questions whirled around in her mind, all centered on finding the two of them together. There was only one way she could learn the answer. Dawn started forward, circling around the mime to approach them.

Randy wasn't aware of her presence until he happened to look up and noticed Slater staring at someone. He turned, seeing her when she was nearly to him. Surprise flickered across his face.

"Mom. What are you doing here?" Randy voiced it, then seemed to suddenly realize who else was standing with him, and looked anxiously from one to the other.

The gray of Slater's eyes was as hard as flintstone. It was difficult for Dawn to reply normally when she was so aware of the bitter anger that had marked the end of their last meeting. There was a prickling sensitivity along her nerve ends.

"I've been looking all over for you, Randy. Your grandparents waited supper for nearly an hour," she informed him, capable of only a mild rebuke now that she saw the reason that had detained him.

"Gosh, Mom," Randy frowned in sincere con-
trition, and looked guiltily at the half-eaten
conch fritter that had taken the edge off his
appetite. "I didn't realize it was that late. I'm
sorry."

"I'm sure you are," Dawn conceded. "The next
time you need to keep better track of the time."

"I will. It's just that—" he paused to throw a
glance at the silent man beside him, "—we've
been talking . . . about things," he finished
lamely.

"I know." It was a noncommittal answer, but it
finally turned her attention to Slater.

All the while she had been talking to Randy
she had been conscious of the angry vibrations
emanating from Slater. She was conscious, too,
of her slightly disheveled appearance. She
wasn't the picture of sophistication and confi-
dence that she had been this afternoon.

Wisps of hair were curling damply against the
sides of her face and along her neck. Her skin
was glowing with a fine sheen of perspiration
after the blocks she'd walked looking for Randy.
The brevity of her white shorts showed the
shapely length of her tanned legs and the slim
curve of her hips. The loden green tank top did
more than expose her golden-brown shoulders.
The knit material clung to her skin, outlining the
points of her breasts that had hardened under his
regard.

Instead of being proud that her figure hadn't
sagged and lost its firmness after childbirth,
Dawn was self-conscious of her definitely female

shape. It wasn't as if she had dressed this way in an attempt to lure Slater's interest. She hadn't even known Randy was with him. Yet, after his accusation this afternoon that she wanted him back, her scantily clad appearance might be interpreted as an attempt to arouse his prurient interest.

"I hope you weren't worried about me, Mom," Randy said anxiously.

Dawn didn't respond to that directly because she knew she had been unjustly angry. It hadn't been a ploy to gain her attention that had kept him from coming home, but the excitement of finally meeting his natural father and being with him that had made Randy forget the time.

"I knew you didn't have lights or reflectors on your bike," she said as an excuse for her concern. "I didn't want you riding it after dark."

"I'm sorry, Mom." He shifted uncomfortably, shrugging his shoulders as he glanced down at his feet.

Through the entire conversation, Slater had remained silent. Now he turned slightly at an angle that brought him near to Dawn and facing Randy.

"The sun is on its way down. You'd better get your bike and start for your grandparents' house," he advised Randy in a calm, even voice.

His attention was focused entirely on Randy so there was no warning as his fingers clamped themselves around her wrist. Her pulse skittered wildly under the firm grip of his hand. She stiffened in raw tension, but didn't pull away.

She understood the silent message conveyed by his detaining hand. Randy was to leave, but she was to remain. She felt hot and cold all at the same time, dreading the conversation that was to come yet hoping at last he would listen to her.

"I told them not to wait supper for you," she said to Randy, fighting to keep the nervousness out of her voice. "So when you get home, you'll have to fix yourself something to eat. Don't let your grandmother do it for you either."

He had started to take a step, then stopped, reading between the lines of her remarks. "Aren't you coming, Mom?" Randy frowned.

"I'll be home a little later on," she said. "You just be sure to go straight home."

"I will," he promised, but he looked at her a little uncertainly before finally trotting away.

For long, charged seconds, she watched the point where Randy had disappeared into the crowd on the pier until she finally saw him exiting the dock. All the while, she was conscious of the clamp of Slater's strong fingers keeping her at his side.

When she was satisfied Randy intended to obey her directions, she let her glance slide to Slater's profile etched against a purpling sky. He, too, was observing Randy's departure. The questions she had wanted to ask when she'd first seen them together came rushing back.

"Why—?" Dawn stopped and chose another. "How did Randy find—"

"He saw my car parked in the driveway of the Van de Veere house. He was waiting for me when

I drove back to the office," Slater answered her question before she had a chance to finish it. "He'd already looked the address up in the phone book."

"But how did he know—" She was frowning.

"He overheard you making the appointment with my secretary to meet me there." Again, he accurately guessed what she had been about to ask.

"So he had been listening," Dawn murmured to herself, remembering her uncertainty at the time. Instead of relaxing his hold on her wrist, he tightened it and started forward, forcing her to come with him. "You're hurting me," she protested and twisted her arm, trying to force him to loosen his grip rather than actually attempting to break it.

The pressure eased slightly, letting the blood flow again. "We're going to my office—where we can talk in private," Slater announced in a voice that was deadly flat.

There was no opportunity to voice her agreement with his desire for a less public place to hold their discussion. He obviously took it for granted. Dawn quickened her steps to keep pace with his longer strides as he led the way through the crowd of evening revelers.

It was a relatively short distance from Mallory Pier to his office. When they reached it, he released her wrist to unlock the door. In a show of her own free will, Dawn barely gave him a chance to open the door before she was brushing past him to walk inside so he would know this was a conversation she sought, and not one that was being forced on her.

She paused inside the small reception area, unsure which door opened into his private office. Slater extended a hand, indicating the one directly in front of her. She walked to it and went inside. Her curious glance inspected the room, Key West in flavor with its trophy-sized marlin mounted and hanging on a wall. There was an airy openness to the room with its whitewashed walls and unshuttered windows. She noted, too, the framed plaques and awards scattered around that attested to his success and contributions to the community.

The top of his desk was cleared, except for a stack of telephone messages in the center of it. Slater ignored them and walked to a rattan table that concealed a small, counter-high refrigerator. He removed a container of ice cubes and dropped two into a glass, then splashed some bourbon over the top of them. Turning, he glanced at Dawn, a raised eyebrow inquiring whether she wanted a drink.

"No, thank you," she refused and remained standing when Slater showed no intention of taking a seat.

He downed half the bourbon in one swallow, then studied the rest. The continued silence produced a heightening tension that became harder to break the longer it lasted. Dawn didn't feel it was her place to speak first. He had refused to listen to her when she had tried to tell him about

Randy this afternoon. Pride insisted he had to ask for the explanation this time.

Slater gave her a long, measuring look. "Don't you think you're a bit old to go running around in public like that?" he criticized.

Stung, Dawn retorted, "Since when is a woman old at thirty?" But she reached up to unconsciously loosen the string binding her hair in its ponytail and combed it free with her fingers.

He watched the action, especially the way the upward reach of her arm stretched the knit fabric of the tanktop across her breasts and their button-hard nipples. The sight disturbed him more than he cared to admit.

"I wasn't referring to your hairstyle," Slater murmured dryly. "There's something innocent about a teenager running around braless. An older woman ends up looking cheap and easy."

"That's one man's opinion." Dawn refused to be drawn into a debate over the issue. His opinion of her was so low he'd find fault with her no matter how conservatively she was dressed. "I doubt if you'd approve of anything I wore. This afternoon you were critical because I wasn't dressed in black."

"You can't claim to look like a widow mourning the death of her husband—not in that outfit with all your assets on display," he snapped in disgust.

"I thought we were here to discuss Randy," she fired back. "If all you want to talk about is the way I dress, then I don't see any point in continuing this conversation." She turned on her heel, knowing he wouldn't let her leave.

"Dammit! You know it's Randy." The admission was reluctantly pulled from him.

Slowly Dawn turned back to face him. This time his gaze swung away from the steadiness of hers. "He is your son," she reaffirmed what Slater hadn't been willing to listen to earlier in the day.

"Did you put him up to it?" Slater swirled the bourbon in his glass.

"Up to what?" she frowned.

"Did you put him up to waiting for me here at the office after we talked today?" Slater elaborated on his question, eyeing her in a sidelong look.

"No, I did not." Her denial was forceful and indignant. "It was all Randy's idea. I knew nothing about it, and if I had, I would have prevented it."

"Why?" His head came up as he demanded an explanation of her statement.

"Because I didn't want him to meet you until we had come to some kind of understanding," Dawn stated, protective of her child.

"An understanding about what?" Slater challenged. "The identity of his father? Granted, I thought you were lying to me this afternoon, but I am capable of accepting the evidence of my own eyes. There isn't much doubt that he's my son. Even Jeeter saw the resemblance."

She was momentarily distracted by the familiarity of the name before she remembered the crusty fishing guide, Jeeter Jones. Then her thoughts focused back on the issue at hand.

"Until this afternoon, it never occurred to me that you might deny the possibility you had fathered my child," Dawn admitted. "I never thought there would be any question about that." She paused to draw a breath, glancing down at her hands. "But I knew how much you despised me. It doesn't matter how you feel about me, but I'm not going to let you try to get back at me by hurting Randy. I won't let you take out your anger on him. "

A silent rage trembled through him before Slater finally exploded. "For eleven years, you keep the existence of our son a secret from me! My son! You've kept him from me all this time— and you stand there and justify it by saying you are afraid I'll hurt him?! My own child?!"

His outrage put her fears to rest, even making them appear foolish in retrospect, but they had been very real to her for a long time.

"I didn't know how you'd react when you found out," she admitted. "And I didn't want to take any chances of Randy being hurt." She felt almost weak with relief. "It could have been easy for you to use him as a weapon against me."

Slater was slowly bringing his temper under control. He bolted down the rest of his drink and turned to refill the glass, a whiteness continuing to show along the taut line of his mouth. "If you weren't the mother of my son, I think I could kill you for even suggesting I'd do that," he muttered thickly.

But his threat struck a responsive chord in her own feelings and reassured as opposed to frightening her. This strong love for their son was a primitive bond they shared in common. It suddenly became easier to talk.

"I suppose he asked you a lot of questions today," Dawn surmised.

"No. Mostly Randy just talked . . . about himself, school, things he liked to do . . . and I just listened." He stared at his drink, but didn't taste it. "How long has he known that Simpson wasn't his father?" It was close to being a loaded question.

"Since I felt he was old enough to understand. He was around five years old at the time. I explained only as much as I thought he could comprehend, then waited for him to come to me with questions when they occurred to him. So actually, his knowledge of you was gained over a period of years."

"He's known about me all this time. And you're only now bothering to inform me about his existence. Didn't I have the right to know before this?" he accused harshly.

"Yes, you did." But it had taken her a long time to arrive at that conclusion.

"Then why didn't you tell me?" Slater demanded. "For eleven years, another man raised my son. There's eleven years out of his life that I'll never have!" He was growing angry at the injustice of it. "I thought there wasn't any more you could take from me. But you took my son!"

"If I had known I was pregnant with our child, I never would have married Simpson," Dawn countered to deflect some of his anger. "But I didn't know it. And when I discovered I was pregnant, I thought it was my husband's baby. And I was glad, because I was finally giving something back to him after all I had taken."

"So you passed him off as Simpson's child," he accused.

"I believed he was." She remembered how happy she had been when the doctor had confirmed her suspicions only a couple of months after the wedding. She had been so eager to tell Simpson the news, knowing that he had given up any hope of having an heir and guessing how much he secretly hoped for one whenever he played with his nieces or nephews. She recalled, also, how confused she had been when he had failed to express delight at her news.

"How long before you realized he wasn't?" Slater wanted to know.

"Almost right away," Dawn admitted with poignant recollection. "Simpson told me." Her mouth twisted with the irony of it. "A week after I told him the happy tidings, he came back to tell me his."

"Which was?"

Chapter Five

"Simpson couldn't have children." Her voice was low with the remembered shock of that moment. "Some childhood fever had left him sterile. It was a small detail he hadn't considered important enough to tell me before the wedding. When I informed him we were expecting a baby, he didn't tell me about his sterility until he had reconfirmed it with his doctor in case some miracle had happened."

"Why didn't you get an annulment?" Slater challenged and watched with narrowed and critical eyes.

"And do what?" Dawn asked, because it had occurred to her at the time. "Come back here to you? Pregnant and divorced? After what I'd done to you, you might not have wanted me back. You might not have believed it was your child I was carrying. Even if you had, how would you have taken care of us? You didn't have a steady job and all you owned was a broken-down old boat and the clothes on your back."

"And you didn't have any faith in my ability to take care of you," he declared grimly, tipping his head back to toss down the second drink. "If I had been Simpson and discovered my loving wife was going to have another's man's child, I would have thrown you out."

"Thank heaven you weren't Simpson," Dawn murmured with a trace of resentment for his callous attitude. "He had more than enough grounds for divorce, but he was willing to forgive and forget."

Only later had she learned that there never had been a divorce in the Lord family, and Simpson had been a great one for upholding the family tradition. Still, even if he had felt honor-bound to continue their marriage, it didn't alter the love and understanding he had shown her, and the kindness he had shown her son. She couldn't have asked more from a man than Simpson had given her.

"So you stayed with him." A humorless sound like a laugh lifted the corners of his mouth, widening it into a derisive smile. "Why not? He was filthy rich. That's why you married him—to get your hands on his money." He lifted his glass in a mock salute. "I never did congratulate you on your success."

Dawn ignored the latter, failing again to correct his impression that she had been left a wealthy widow. "That's why I married him," she admitted. "But his money had very little to do with the reason I stayed with him, beyond assuring my child would be well cared for. After Simpson explained that he couldn't be the father of the child I was carrying, I had to tell him about you. He already knew. I think he even knew why I married him but it didn't matter. You can imagine how I felt."

"No, I can't imagine how you felt." Slater shook his head, his voice running low with contempt. He deliberately refused to understand or even concede she was capable of remorse.

Nothing would be gained by responding to his caustic retort. Dawn felt more could be accomplished by trying to make him understand the reasons behind some of her actions.

"I remember Simpson telling me that, in a way, he was glad he couldn't produce children because he wasn't obligated to make an advantageous business marriage to consolidate wealth since it would require an heir. He was free to marry the girl he loved, which was me." She bowed her head slightly as she spoke. "He loved me enough to accept another man's child into his home. I know you'll find this hard to believe, Slater, but by then, I was tired of hurting people. After hurting so many, I couldn't hurt Simpson more than I already had. I couldn't give him my love, because you had it, but I decided that I could give him happiness. So, yes, I stayed with him—out of a mixture of gratitude and guilt— and I worked at being a good wife to bring him some of the happiness he deserved."

"And you gave him my son," Slater shot the accusation at her, ignoring all else she had told him. "I suppose Simpson passed Randy off as his own."

"No. For Randy's sake, he let him take the

family surname, but Simpson never legally adopted him. And it's your name that is listed as father on his birth certificate," Dawn explained. "Simpson played the role of Dutch uncle to Randy, but he never usurped your position as his father. He was adamant about that."

Her answer brought a moment's silence. When Slater finally spoke, it was with considerably less heat and bitterness. "I guess I owe him something for that." He set his empty glass on the rattan table and squared around to face her. "Which brings us back to Randy, and what's to be done now."

"Not having a father never bothered Randy too much while Simpson was alive." She threaded her fingers together, spreading them and studying the straight patterns they made. "He needs a father. He needs you." She looked at him, folding her fingers together in a prayerful attitude that asked for a truce between them.

His gray eyes glittered in a cold, calculating study of her. "I can't help wondering why you waited until after Simpson was dead before you suddenly decided that Randy needed a father. It can't be that you were waiting until he died. The man's been dead for more than two months."

"Do you think I should have flown out here the day after his funeral?" Dawn bristled at his veiled attack. "There was a small matter of putting affairs in order, not to mention the shock of losing someone I had grown to care about."

"Of course." But it was a response that mocked her explanation. Slater wandered idly toward her, that cool, assessing gaze of his continuing to study her. "At first I had the crazy idea that you'd come back for a much more personal reason. I suppose it shows the size of my ego that I thought you were here to see if we couldn't get back together again. The second time you were going to marry for love—that's what you told me the morning you left. And I wanted to believe that you still cherished some love for me." His voice was growing harder and colder.

How could she tell him that she did when she didn't know how much of her desire was rooted in nostalgia? Both of them had changed so much. It wasn't possible to feel the same. But there was unquestionably smoke coming from an old fire and the ashes were still hot.

"Then I found out about Randy," he said in a tone that indicated the knowledge had changed his thinking. "So you're here, claiming he needs a father." His gaze made a slow sweep of her, taking in every curve of her body. "And there you stand—a sexy, young widow with money to burn and no one to tell her how she should spend it and with eleven years of having to be a good wife behind her. A half-grown son is bound to be an encumbrance."

"That's not true," Dawn protested, stung by his implication.

"Isn't it?" Slater challenged, stopping in front of her. "You say he needs a father. Are you planning to dump him on me so you can go out and have your fun? It must be difficult to g husband-hunting with a brat in tow. How much easier it is to pawn him off onto someone else."

She was trembling with anger, too incensed to voice any kind of denial to such totally false and denigrating accusations. The recourse left to her was completely instinctive, the impulse to strike the words from his mouth.

The lightning arc of her hand aimed for his cheek, striking it with all the force she could put behind it. The blow turned his head to the side, the impact stinging the palm of her hand. Her own temper made her indifferent to the retaliating anger that darkened his expression. If anything, she felt satisfaction seeing the white mark on his jaw slowly turning red where she had struck him.

Dawn had acted with no thought of the consequences, forgetting that violence was invariably answered with violence. She was forcibly reminded of it when her arms were seized and she was yanked roughly against him, his fingers digging into her soft flesh. The murderous light smouldering in his eyes brought a flicker of alarm to her expression.

The glimpse of it made Slater pause. An expression that was both wry and bitter with regret swept across his features, but his gaze continued to bore into her. The grip of his hands had pulled her onto her toes and arched her body against the length of his. Sensitive nerve endings picked up the sensation of her bare thighs pressed to the cotton texture of his slacks and the solidness of his hip bones ground against hers. The peaks of her breasts were flattened to the hard wall of his chest. Dawn was hardly drawing a breath while her heart beat unevenly, not certain what would happen next.

His mouth thinned into a grim line as he released a disgusted breath that warmed her face. "Ours always was a very *physical* relationship," Slater muttered thickly as if that explained this mutual show of violence. "We still can't seem to communicate on any other level."

Her glance slid to the discolored area on his cheek where she had hit him, and taken pleasure in it. Dawn was sorry now, but—as always it seemed—her regret came too late. Her hands rested loosely on his rib cage, no longer resisting his closeness. Even as she silently acknowledged the accuracy of his statement, she was cognizant of the necessary qualification it needed.

"But we never used to try to hurt each other," she reminded him.

"No, we didn't," he agreed.

A darkness blazed in his eyes, but it was no longer sparked by anger. She could feel the burning heat of it moving over her face and neck. It warmed her in a way that was all too familiar. Without seeming to loosen his grip, his hold on her shifted. One hand curled into her hair at the back of her neck while the other glided down her back.

A half-smothered groan came from his throat as he bent his head toward her. Dawn smelled the whiskey on his breath and turned her lips from him at the last second, letting his mouth graze her cheek.

"You're crazy drunk," she warned him, not because she didn't want his kiss. She did. But she remembered too clearly how their brief, torrid embrace this afternoon had turned him bitter and angry with regret. She didn't want to put either of them through that again.

"Yes, I'm crazy drunk." His mouth, his nose, his chin kept moving over the side of her averted face, nuzzling and exploring what territory was accessible to him. "I'm like a wino who's been on the wagon for eleven years. Then he finds a bottle of wine—the same vintage as the one he took his last drink from—and he wonders if it still has that same wild and sweet bouquet. One little taste, he says." He lipped her ear, drawing a shudder of pleasure from Dawn, and took the lobe between his teeth in a sensual love-bite. "One little taste and that's all. He won't take any more, so he thinks. But all it takes is one taste, and the wino discovers he won't be satisfied until he has the whole bottle." His mouth hovered against the corner of her lips. "You're my bottle of wine, Dawn. I've already had the first taste— the one kiss. I won't be satisfied until I've taken it all."

It was a husky entreaty to give it to him. Inside she was a trembling mass, needing him as much as he claimed to need her. It didn't take much effort to turn that short inch to bring her lips into contact with his mouth. At first their mouths brushed over each other in a feather kiss that heightened the sensitivity of their lips.

When the anticipation level had reached a fever-pitch that had them straining against each other, his mouth rolled onto hers, opening to consume it whole. Her reaching hands went around his middle and flattened across his back, trying to defy physical laws and bring them still closer together.

For endless, whirling minutes, they kissed passionately, devouring each other, his hands roaming, touching, and molding her to fit to his hard contours. When their lips finally untangled so each could draw a labored breath, there was the rawness of dissatisfaction. Slater buried his face in the curve of her neck where her pulse was throbbing madly.

"You don't know the hell I've gone through," he muttered with an ache in his voice, "knowing you legally belonged in another man's bed—and picturing you lying in his arms."

"And you don't know what the agony was like for me—" she whispered to let him know he wasn't the only one who had been haunted by images, "—lying with him and having him touch me and kiss me all the while wishing it was you. Worse, I never stopped wishing it was you."

"What are you wishing now?" His hand had found its way to the bare skin at the small of her back. Slater lifted his head to bring his face inches above hers while he studied her. The black pupils of his eyes had widened until only a silver ring showed around them.

"I'm wishing that you'd love me." In every sense of the word, she meant it, but it seemed unnecessary to elaborate.

It was a wish that seemed destined, at last, to be fulfilled as the crushing weight of his mouth rocked onto her lips. They parted to invite a deepening of the kiss to its fullest intimacy. When her feet were lifted off the floor by his carrying arms, Dawn felt weightless.

She was barely conscious of the lengthening shadows outside the office windows as the darkness of dusk settled over the building. It was only a short distance to the sofa from where they had been standing. Slater set her down on a cushion, his hands lifting the bottom of her tanktop and pulling it over her head as they came away.

Her deep blue eyes were heavy with desire as he leaned toward her and let a hand slide onto her naked breast. She was reaching for him to draw him down on the cushion with her as she lay back. It was imperative that nothing come between them—not the past or the future—or the silken shirt covering his chest from her seeking fingers.

While his lips made exciting forays from her throat to her maturely rounded breasts, she was tugging at the shirt buttons to unfasten them. As soon as his shirt was hanging open, her hands slipped inside to feel the heat of his skin. It was a sensation she didn't have a chance to enjoy for long as his teasing tongue had her writhing with another need.

Actions and sensations all began to flow into

one another—his hand pushing the elastic waist-band of her shorts over her hipbone; the searing taste of his kiss drinking deeply of her love; the weight of his flatly muscled body settling onto her; naked flesh against naked flesh; and the golden fire in her loins consuming all thought but the pleasure that came from giving love and receiving it. The sound of her name coming from his lips became her only touch with reality. It was repeated over and over, interspliced with love words that were too quickly lost.

How long she lay afterwards in the possessive clasp of his circling arms, their bodies squeezed together by the narrow width of the sofa, Dawn couldn't have said. But in its own way, this holding of each other was equally as pleasing as the sexual gratification had been. His musky body smell was all around her, warm and enveloping.

"It's been so long since I've felt like this." She traced the hard edge of his jaw with the tip of her finger, feeling the faint bristle that had scraped the skin around her mouth and left it tender.

Slater lightly captured her fingers and lifted them to his mouth, drawing her glance to its male line as he pressed her fingers to it. When she looked at him fully, his expression seemed unnaturally somber. He held her gaze, the gray of his eyes probing in its search for something.

"You got your wish, didn't you?" His comment sounded casual. Dawn wasn't able to detect any hint of bitter mockery.

She nodded once. "It was your wish, too, wasn't it?" she asked.

"Yes." Slater glanced at her ringless fingers. "I've wished for this a long time." His look was almost gentle, a tinge of sadness in it, but no regret that Dawn could see. A muscle flexed in the arm she was lying on. "Move," he said. "My arm's going to sleep."

Reluctantly she propped herself up on an elbow to take her weight off his arm. Instead of merely changing position, Slater sat up and reached for his trousers. She released an inaudible sigh. This moment of supreme closeness had to come to an end sometime, but she had wanted it to last a little longer. But no one could hold on to this rare kind of happiness forever.

By the time she had pulled the hem of her tanktop down around her waist, Slater was standing by the desk. He switched on a tall lamp, chasing away the intimacy of near darkness with the sudden glare of light. Shirtless, the upper half of his body had a sun-bronzed sheen to it that rippled with the play of his muscles as he turned his back to her and reached for something on the desk.

"Cigarette?" he asked with a glance over his shoulder.

"No thanks." Dawn bent down to slip on her sandals, hooking a finger in the back strap to ease it over her heel. She heard the snap of a cigarette lighter, and the click of it being shut.

When she straightened, he was leaning against

the edge of the desk, half-sitting on it while he watched her. There was something unnerving about his absent stare. She sensed that he had withdrawn from her and become preoccupied with his own secret thoughts. She couldn't stand not knowing what was going on in his head.

"Penny for your thoughts?" she said with a quick smile to make her curiosity appear more casual.

His mouth twitched almost into a smile. "You could have bought them for that once, but I'm worth more than that now." The drawled response eased much of her concern.

"I noticed all your business trophies on the walls." Dawn glanced briefly at the plaques of achievement.

"I don't claim to be in Simpson Lord's league yet," Slater stated dryly and flicked the ash from the end of his cigarette. "But he had a couple of generations' headstart on me."

It had not been spoken entirely in jest. There was a competitive edge in the words, as if the worth of a man was judged by the amount of money in his bankbook. Dawn had learned the hard way it was a false standard to use in the search for happiness. And she didn't want Slater to think she still believed that was important.

"That doesn't matter to me, Slater," she insisted quickly.

Again his mouth slanted with a crooked smile. "That's right. This time it's for love, isn't it?" he mocked. Before she could respond to that vague jibe, the muted ring of a telephone sounded in the outer office area. He picked up the receiver on his desk. "MacBride," he said into the phone. Without speaking again to the calling party, he straightened from the desk and held out the receiver to her. "It's for you."

Briefly startled by his announcement, she crossed quickly to the desk to take the phone from his hand. "Hello?"

"Dawn?" It was her mother's voice on the other end of the wire. "I'm sorry to call you but it was getting so late and I—" She trailed off lamely without completing the sentence.

"It's all right," Dawn assured her that she wasn't upset by the phone call.

"I just wasn't sure how late you would be— whether I should wait up for you or leave the housekey under the mat outside the door," her mother explained so Dawn wouldn't think she was trying to dictate what hour she should come home.

"I'll be there shortly," Dawn promised, guessing that Randy was probably as anxious as her mother to find out what had transpired during the long discussion with Slater. She couldn't very well tell either of them how much had been said without words.

"All right. I hope I didn't interrupt anything important," her mother added.

"You didn't. Good-bye." She waited until her mother had echoed the word before hanging up the phone. She glanced at Slater as he paused near the desk to grind out his cigarette butt in the ashtray. "That was—"

"—your mother," he interrupted to finish the sentence and identify the voice he'd heard.

"You recognized her voice," she realized.

"I suppose the clucking mother hen was checking up on her missing chick," Slater guessed with a smoothness that bothered her.

"In a way," Dawn admitted, and glanced at the darkness outside the window panes. "It's later than I realized."

He looked at his watch. "Past your parents' bedtime," he acknowledged. "I suppose they're anxious to lock up the doors and turn in."

"Yes." There was something about this conversation that she didn't like, although it seemed innocent enough on the surface.

"Do you suppose they've guessed what we've been doing all this time?" he asked, then answered his own question. "I don't imagine they have. They were always a few minutes late on the scene, whether it was your mother waiting on the porch five minutes before you were supposed to be home or your father not finding us on my boat until the next morning. Was that the night Randy was conceived?"

He was dredging up too many memories and appearing to taunt her with them. Her mind was whirling, trying to keep pace with the changing direction of his sentences.

"It must have been," she nodded.

Slater turned from her and she found herself facing the muscled smoothness of his tanned back. "You'd better go," he said. "You promised your mother you'd be home shortly."

"Yes." But she didn't make any move to leave, not wanting to go now that everything between them suddenly seemed so unsettled. "Slater." She came up to his side and laid her hand on the taut, sinewed muscles of his upper arm.

With grudging slowness, he faced her and looked down the straight bridge of his nose at her. There was indecision in his eyes, an inner war being waged with himself. Dawn swayed toward him, in some way wanting to reassure him.

The little movement brought his arms around her to catch her to him, and gather her hard to his body. His mouth was coming down as he muttered roughly, "Damn you for twisting me up into knots like this."

There was something hard and demanding in his rough kiss that hadn't been there before, as if he was trying to exorcise her ghost from his system. Dawn pulled away from his mouth and stared at him in hurt and half-angry confusion.

Instantly he released her and moved away, but she had a glimpse of the darkening frown gathering on his forehead.

"I'm sorry, Dawn." But he didn't say for what. "Go," he urged with absent gruffness. "Before your mother starts getting worried."

She hesitated a second more then walked to the door, letting his apology take the place of an explanation for the time being. She had the inner door open and was halfway out of it when Slater added, "I'll talk to you tomorrow."

He tossed the remark after her with an absent

indifference. Dawn saw it as a desire to continue their relationship, however reluctantly it was expressed. There had been a few minutes when she had thought it was going to fall apart all over again.

When she stepped into the clear night, bright stars shone in the sky overhead, and a big, old moon rode high above the horizon. A cool sea breeze drifted off the water to scent the languid air. It was a long time since she had noticed such things.

Chapter Six

All the breakfast dishes were washed and returned to their respective places in the kitchen cupboard, except for a coffee cup. It was sitting on the table where her father was still reading the morning paper. Dawn hummed along with the song being played on the radio while she swept the kitchen floor, tapping her father's shoes so he would move his feet and allow the broom to reach the area under him.

Her mother was hurrying around drawing all the window shades and drapes to trap the lingering coolness of the night air inside the house. Randy was outside, playing by the garage. Every once in a while, Dawn heard the basketball hitting the backboard her father had installed above the garage door.

As she swept the dust into a small pile, Dawn was absently amazed at how easily she had reverted to the habit of doing household chores after so many years of having them done for her by others. Maybe she'd tire of them, but right now she didn't resent doing them at all. Maybe that acceptance came with maturity, too.

When she reached for the dustpan, a car roared into the driveway. Instantly the dustpan was forgotten and the broom was hurriedly propped against a cabinet counter as Dawn rushed to the back door. Her face lit up when she saw the shiny black Corvette. She pushed the door open and stepped onto the back stoop. Randy was already running to greet Slater, so she waited there, taking the couple of extra minutes to smooth her watersilk blouse inside the waistband of her tangerine slacks.

There was a suggestion of impatience in the line of his long, muscled body as Slater paused to greet Randy. He smiled, but Dawn noticed the smile didn't reach his eyes. Her expression sobered slightly, her gaze becoming more watchful.

When he started toward the house, his strongly cut features seemed close to wearing a brooding scowl. He looked up to see her standing at the railing around the stoop, and just as quickly, his glance skipped away. Another bad sign. Dawn fought to hold the bitter disappointment and hurt away from her expression.

"Good morning," she greeted him with what she hoped was calmness.

"Morning," he returned, the omission of an adjective making it starkly apparent there was nothing "good" in it as far as he was concerned.

A surge of stubbornness made Dawn confront him with his obviously sour mood. "You're grumpy this morning," she challenged to identify the reason.

His eyes were like gray stones, hard and impenetrable when they finally met her searching gaze. The lack of any emotion in them seemed to confirm her suspicion that Slater was wishing last night hadn't happened for them, regardless of what he'd said at the time. Her lips compressed into a taut line.

"I guess I haven't had my morning quota of caffeine," Slater countered her challenge with an obvious lie.

"We still have some coffee left over from breakfast. Why don't you come in and have a cup?" Dawn invited, conscious that Randy was trailing along at Slater's heels, making any open discussion impossible while he was there.

"Fine." It was a clipped answer of acceptance. Pivoting, Dawn led the way into the house, feeling the tension mount in her system. Both her parents were in the kitchen when they entered it. Slater had obviously been the subject of their conversation since both fell into a guilty silence.

"Have a seat." Dawn coolly waved a hand at the chairs around the kitchen table. "I'll pour your coffee."

"Hello, Slater." Her father wasn't sure how to handle the situation, whether to greet him as a longtime family friend or a mere acquaintance. Dawn had been very circumspect about the information she'd given her mother last night, downplaying her meeting with Slater. Now she was glad she hadn't sounded too optimistic. "I'd ask how business is—" her father continued

"—but every time I turn around I hear 'MacBride owns this' or you sold that or you're making a ton of money from something else."

"I can't complain." But Slater didn't return the courtesy by inquiring how her father was doing, nor did he offer any encouragement for the conversation to continue.

As Dawn took a cup from the cupboard and filled it with coffee, she heard the scrape of a chair leg. Randy had brought the basketball into the house and was absently bouncing it on the linoleum floor. It was nearly as irritating as drumming fingers.

"Not in the house, Randy," she reminded him as she carried Slater's cup of coffee to the table.

"Sorry, Mom. I forgot." He hooked the ball under his arm and hovered next to Slater's chair. "Do you wanta come out and watch me shoot a few baskets after you drink your coffee? I'm pretty good." Randy seemed to be the only one who wasn't conscious of the brittle atmosphere in the kitchen.

"We'll see." Slater avoided a commitment.

"I'm on my way to the grocery store," her mother announced. "Is there anything you need, Dawn?"

"No." She walked back to the kitchen counter to pour herself a cup of the strong, black coffee.

There was the rustle of the newspaper being folded and set aside as her father took a clue from his wife's departure. "Got some work I need to get finished in the garage," he said and followed his wife out the back door.

"You should see the stuff Gramps makes in his workshop." It didn't occur to Randy that his presence might not be wanted. "He's been letting me help him, and showing me how to do stuff. I found this piece of driftwood that we're going to make into a lamp. It's got a real weird shape. Do you want to come out and see it?"

"Not now!" His voice was harsh with impatience.

Dawn saw the hurt frown cloud Randy's features. She was instantly angry. "Slater," she spoke his name in sharp rebuke.

This time the angry impatience on his features was directed at himself. He sliced a grimly apologetic glance at Randy. "I'm sorry. I had no cause to snap at you." Slater sighed heavily and rubbed a hand across his forehead. "I'm not feeling in the best of moods this morning."

"That's okay." Randy was quick to dismiss his rudeness as he worked to acquire a pseudo-adult air for a man-to-man comment. "What cha got? A hangover?"

Slater's gaze flicked briefly to Dawn. "You could say that," he murmured with a wry, biting twist of humor to his mouth.

The look immediately reminded her of the analogy he'd made between himself and an alcoholic. An auburn brow shot up. "From too much vintage wine?" she taunted coolly and sat across the table from him.

"Yes." There was considerably less humor in the curve of his mouth, his eyes darkening in withdrawal from this word-game. He continued to study her as he spoke to his son. "Why don't you run outside, Randy, so I can talk privately with your mother. I'll be out after I finish my coffee."

Randy didn't like being excluded again, but his relationship with his father was too new for him to risk testing it by refusing to leave. Glumly he walked to the door.

"Don't be too long," was the closest he came to a protest.

Keeping her eyes downcast, Dawn looked into the mirror-black surface of her coffee and waited for the sound of the door latching securely behind Randy. Her nerves felt raw from this constant exposure to Slater's ever-reoccurring resentment toward her.

"We never did get around to having our talk last night," he said, breaking the heavy silence that had descended on the room with Randy's departure.

"I guess we didn't." She continued to stare at her cup. For a while last night, she hadn't thought there was anything left to discuss. Obviously she was wrong.

"Just what is it you want from me?" Slater demanded.

Her head came up sharply, her gaze flying to the chilling set of his hard features. "If you have to ask—" Dawn checked the angry words.

Nothing would be gained by losing her temper and lashing out at him. It was apparent that he was shutting out those moments when love had blazed so brilliantly. She struggled to do the same and respond to his questions as if it hadn't happened.

"I want you to be a father to Randy—to be there when he needs you." That had been her original desire when she had returned to Key West. She hadn't dared hope for more than that. Foolishly she had begun to believe there could be.

"Are you planning to stay here?" He sounded like an interrogator who had no stake in her answer.

"Yes—providing, of course, that we come to some kind of truce where Randy is concerned." Too agitated to remain seated, Dawn stood up and carried her full cup of coffee back to the counter by the pot, setting it down. "Naturally, I don't intend to live with my parents. That's why I was interested in purchasing the Van de Veere house—providing the price was reasonable." She kept her back to the table, unable to look at him while she endured this farcical conversation. "How much is it?"

When she turned, she was startled to discover Slater was standing only a few feet from her. He had moved so quietly she hadn't been aware he'd followed her.

After he had quoted a price well within range of what she could afford to pay, he added, "So we won't have to waste time haggling over the price, I'll drop it another two thousand."

"Sold." It was totally a reflex movement that prompted Dawn to extend a hand to shake on the deal.

Slater just looked at it, then slowly raised his

glance to her face. White and trembling from this deliberate affront, Dawn held her head high, falling back on pride now that all else had failed her. But moisture gathered in her eyes to blur her vision and there was a traitorous quiver of her chin.

"Damn you," she cursed hoarsely, and swung away to grip the edge of the counter. "And damn you for being a man. You're schooled from the cradle not to show your feelings. And girls are encouraged to cry when they're hurt. It isn't fair," Dawn protested in a choked voice, and brushed impatiently at a tear that slipped off her lashes. "What happened? Last night I thought—"

"Do you think one night with you can make up for the thousands I spent alone?" He bitterly hurled the angry words to cut off her sentence.

Her head jerked as if she had been slapped. But the demand served to check her tears. "No, I don't." Her voice lost its husky waver although it remained tight. "It happened too soon. I should have known it did. You've hated me for so long. Not even you can reverse directions overnight." The corners of her mouth curled into a sad, laughing smile. "There's something in that old saying about 'the cold light of day,' isn't there?"

"Maybe it's myself I'm not liking very much this morning," Slater offered grimly. Dawn turned slowly to look at him and discover what he meant by that statement. He moved closer, stopping when his legs brushed against hers, in effect pinning her between himself and the counter. "I had sworn if you ever came back, I wouldn't have anything to do with you. I wasn't even going to give you the time of day. It lowers a man's opinion of himself when he learns he hasn't the strength to resist the temptation of a woman's body." Self-derision deepened the corners of his mouth. "And I'm too old and too experienced to claim that you seduced me. I was more than willing—I was eager."

"Now you're sorry." That's what hurt.

"I don't know what I am," he declared with a grim shake of his head. "One minute I want to hurt you before you can hurt me, and in the next, I just want to love you."

Dawn wished he wasn't standing so near. She didn't want to feel the muscled columns of his thighs or the slight thrust of his hips. It was all too evocative and intimate.

"I'll tell you what," she began. "Until you decide which way you want it to be, why don't you go back on the wagon?" She stepped sideways to end the contact with him although her senses continued to clamor from it. "In the meantime, we'll keep everything on a strictly business level."

"That's roughly what I was going to suggest," Slater said, and didn't sound too happy that she had proposed it first.

"About the house—how long will it take to have the papers drawn so we can close the sale?" Now that she had changed the subject, Dawn stayed with it. "There's no need to discuss terms. I'll pay cash."

"Of course," he murmured dryly. "I can write up the contract today, but you'll need the abstract examined and brought up to date."

"How long before I can take possession?" she asked.

"As far as I'm concerned, you can move into the house this afternoon if you want. All the paper work and deeds should be ready within a week." Slater paused, studying her a second. "You don't have to buy the house. It's just sitting empty. You and Randy are welcome to live in it—for as long as you want."

"For nothing?" Dawn was certain there had to be some kind of strings attached.

"For nothing," he assured her.

"No thanks," she refused his apparently generous offer. "I'd rather not be under any obligation to you. I prefer to buy it rather than have people talking about me as Slater MacBride's kept woman."

"Randy is my son," Slater reminded her. "I offered the house so I could contribute something toward his support. I was not trying to put you in my debt."

"Perhaps you weren't," she conceded. "But just the same, I'd rather purchase the house outright. We'll probably move into it as soon as possible."

"I can arrange to have a crew go over there and clean the place up for you," he said.

"There's no need. I'll handle it myself," Dawn insisted. "I'll stop by your office early this afternoon to sign the necessary papers and make a down payment. You can leave them with your secretary—along with the doorkey."

"I'll do that." It was all very curt and professional. "I'll go out and see Randy before I leave."

Dawn watched him walk out the door. On the surface, it seemed to be a sound and workable proposal, but she knew it was doomed to failure. They shared too many intimate memories to ever sustain a business relationship without personalities interfering. They were just kidding themselves.

Dawn had put most of her household and personal possessions in storage before she left Texas. After she had signed the papers for the house, she arranged to have them shipped to Key West. While she waited for them to arrive, there was a great deal of work to be done on the property, both outside and in. Viewing it as a kind of therapy to take her mind off Slater, Dawn threw herself into it with all her energies.

The overgrown yard was chosen as the first task. Randy teased her that she intended to wage war with it when he saw the tools she had raided from her father's equipment shed. There was the usual assemblage of garden tools, such as rakes, hoes, and spades, plus more lethal items—hatchets, machetes, and a double-bladed axe. She loaded them into a wheelbarrow and, together, she and Randy wheeled it over to their new house in the cool of early morning.

Dressed in combat gear consisting of long-sleeved shirts, sturdy denims, boots, and gloves to protect their bodies from the sharp and sometimes thorny underbrush, they attacked the front yard in earnest, using the sidewalk as their route of entry. By late morning, they had made a sizable and hard-fought dent in it. But the heat and the humidity were beginning to wear them down.

Randy had stripped down to the waist, sweat streaming down his shoulders and wetting the thick hair on his forehead. A kerchief was tied around it, creating a sweatband to keep the stinging perspiration out of his eyes. Another wheelbarrow load of palm fronds and tangled vines had to be pushed to the growing pile of debris in the driveway. The muscles in his young arms bulged as he lifted the handles and began driving it forward.

Hot and frazzled, Dawn leaned on her rake. A scarf was tied around her hair. She tipped her head back and squinted at the sun high overhead, trying to judge the time. She hadn't risked wearing her watch for fear she'd catch it on some brush and lose it. The plan had been to work until noon, then quit before the full heat of the day hit them. It had to be close to that now, she decided.

She shifted her grip on the rake and winced in pain. Gingerly she pulled off the glove on her right hand and examined the blister on her palm.

It looked raw and angry. She heard the rattle of the wheelbarrow as its load was dumped and turned to call to Randy.

"Bring a bandage from the first aid kit when you come." Her voice croaked on a weary note.

Stopping, Randy turned and jogged the short distance to the veranda where the first aid kit and water jug sat side by side in the shade. Dawn marveled at the resiliency of youth that Randy still had the energy to move out of a dragging walk.

Enough of the yard had been cleared to enable her to have only a partially obscured view of the street. A flash of black caught her eye, attracted by the sound of a passing car. Only it wasn't passing. Dawn recognized the black Corvette as it swung into the driveway, just managing to stop short of the brush pile.

Even though Dawn was too tired to care about her appearance, she was conscious of it. Her face was streaked with dust and pollen. Stickers and broken twigs were hooked onto her clothes. In this old shirt of her father's, she knew she looked shapeless. Even the crowning glory of her hair was hidden under the dirty scarf. For some strange reason, it was her chipped nails and blistered palms that bothered her the most. There wasn't time to slip her glove back on, and it would have been too painful anyway, so she simply let her hand hang by her side, hoping he wouldn't notice it.

His brows were drawn together in a frown as

his gaze swept the yard, his long, free-swinging strides carrying him to where she was standing. "Where are your workmen? Have they broken for lunch already?"

"We are the workmen," she said, including Randy with a gesture of her gloved hand as he joined them.

"You aren't planning to clean up this yard by yourselves?" He looked at her as if she'd lost her senses.

Dawn was hot and tired enough to wonder if she had. "We're both young and able-bodied. All it takes is a little muscle."

"A weak mind and a strong back, that's what it takes," Slater corrected with a trace of exasperation.

"A little physical labor doesn't hurt anybody," she insisted, and smiled briefly at her son. "Besides, this is going to be our new home. We have to put some effort into making it that." She felt it would be a good lesson for Randy; instill in him a sense of ownership because he had helped with it.

"Here's your bandage, Mom." He offered it to her.

"Physical labor doesn't hurt anybody, huh?" Slater mocked and took the bandage from Randy. His seeking glance noticed the gloveless hand at her side. "A blister?" he guessed.

"Yes. It's just a little sore." She wouldn't admit that it was throbbing painfully since it had been exposed to the air.

Turning her hand palm-upward, she showed him the fiery red sore. His gaze flicked sharply to her face. "You crazy little fool," he muttered angrily under his breath. "You'll be lucky if you don't get infection in it."

"It isn't that bad." But Dawn winced as his finger probed around the edges of it, his touch basically gentle although it imparted pain. He firmly held her hand so she couldn't pull it away from him.

"Do you have any antiseptic with you?" he asked.

"In the first aid kit," she nodded.

"Go get it for me, Randy," he ordered. "Before we put a bandage on it, it needs to be cleansed and treated."

As Randy trotted off again, Dawn didn't want to pursue the subject of her blister, certain it would only invite a lecture from Slater. And if she chose to clean the yard herself instead of having it done, it was entirely her own business. But she wasn't in the mood to argue with him over that point.

"Why did you stop by?" she asked. "Do you have the final papers ready for the house?"

"No, they should be finished tomorrow," he said, then explained, "I had the afternoon free so I stopped by your parents' house to see if Randy wanted to go out on the boat with me. I promised to take him snorkeling some time."

"He'd like that." As sticky and overheated as she felt, the invitation sounded heavenly.

"Do you mean he doesn't have to work in the yard this afternoon?" There was a devilish twinkle in his gray eyes that laughingly mocked her.

"Regardless of what you think, I'm not so foolish as to work outside in the heat of the afternoon," Dawn retorted.

"Why don't you come with us?" Slater invited unexpectedly.

"No." Her refusal was quick, perhaps too quick.

"Why not?" he challenged, deliberately argumentative to wear down her resistance. "With Randy along as chaperon, I'll have to lay off the booze." She stiffened self-consciously at the oblique reference to her, knowing full well it was what she had wanted to avoid when she had initially turned down the invitation. "Sorry. I guess that joke was in poor taste."

"It doesn't matter," she murmured.

"I'd still like you to come with us," he said more quietly. "Being the father of a ten-year-old boy is still new to me. It gets a bit awkward between us sometimes. I'm never sure what I should say to him, or what we're supposed to talk about. I think it would be easier on Randy if you came along to smooth out the rough spots."

She listened to the run of his voice, hearing its calm reasoning and persuasive tone. It made sense. Plus it had been years since she had gone snorkeling in these clear waters. The combination made for an irresistible appeal.

"I'll come," she agreed.

Randy came trotting up, slowing to walk heavily the last couple of steps. "I brought the whole kit 'cause I wasn't sure which you wanted," he said to Slater and opened the box to show him the contents.

"How would you like to go snorkeling this afternoon?" Slater asked as he removed a bottle of disinfectant to cleanse the blistered sore.

"Really?" Randy perked up with interest.

"Your mother's going to come with us." He doused the area as Dawn hissed in a breath at the burning sting it made.

"Great!" His enthusiasm at the news was a total endorsement of the plan.

Slater dabbed on some antiseptic before pressing the adhesive bandage over the sore. "Get all these tools put away and I'll give you a ride home so you can get cleaned up and ready to go."

In record time it seemed, the car was rolling to a stop in her parents' driveway. The motor idled while Slater waited for them to climb out.

"I'll be back in an hour," he said.

"We'll be ready," Dawn promised, although it just barely gave them time to shower, change, and grab a bite of lunch.

As he backed out of the driveway, she curved an arm around Randy's shoulders and turned them both toward the house. When the sound of the motor had faded away, Randy tipped his head back to look at her with an anxious frown.

"Do you think he likes me?" he asked earnestly. "I mean *really* likes me—not just because he should 'cause he's my father." He didn't pause for Dawn to answer. "I want him to like me so much, but sometimes I get all tongue-tied and can't think of anything to say."

Her expression softened. "I'll bet he has that same problem, too."

"I doubt it." He scuffed the toe of his shoe in the gravel.

"I wouldn't worry about it, though," Dawn insisted. "After you get to know each other better, all the awkwardness will go away."

Randy's concern was almost an echo of the sentiment Slater had expressed to her earlier, and confirmed that her presence would be useful. It wasn't something she was just pretending so she would have an excuse to spend an afternoon with Slater.

Chapter Seven

The class of boats tied up at the marina ran the full gamut from sport fishermen with fly bridges to catamarans to houseboats, and anything and everything in between. Dawn silently admired the sleek lines of the thirty-foot cabin cruiser they approached. Slater had already pointed it out as belonging to him.

When she was close enough to read the lettering on the side, she looked at it and laughed, "*Homesick*? What kind of name is that for a boat?"

Instead of being offended, Slater treated her to an indulgent look. "Whenever I get fed up with the business grind and wish I was back lazing around and living off the sea, I take the boat out for a couple of hours—or a couple of days. In other words, I get 'homesick.'"

The explanation silenced her amusement at the name. She knew the drastic change his lifestyle had undergone, and the transition couldn't have been an easy one. She was glad he hadn't severed all ties with the sea. He had loved it so, familiar with its every mood. It was natural for him to miss it, and the *Homesick* would take him back to it whenever he wanted to go.

After they were on board, Slater glanced at Randy. "Do you want to cast off the lines while I start the engines?"

"Sure," he agreed quickly, then snapped a salute. "I mean, aye-aye, sir."

Slater saluted him back, smiling faintly, then headed to the cruiser's bridge area. Dawn followed him, lifting the hair out of her eyes when the wind off the sea blew it across her face. Over her black swimsuit with its swirling tiger-eye pattern, she wore a white lace beach jacket, belted at the waist. She stood to one side of Slater, out of his way, and looked out at the vast expanse of water shimmering under a high sun.

"Whatever happened to the *Seaspray*?" The minute she asked the question, she regretted it. Memories of that boat were all tied up and intertwined with the memory of their romance.

There was a long second when he appeared to be preoccupied checking gauges. "Initially I was going to do something dramatic," he said, looking out to see how Randy was doing but not glancing at her. There was no inflection in his voice that might have indicated he was disturbed by the question. She could just as easily have asked him about the weather. "—like towing her into deep water and sinking her to the bottom, hoping she'd take your ghost with her. In the end, I sold her to some guy from New York and used the money to buy a partnership in a shrimp boat.

From there, I started building my little empire." The last phrase was used wryly, managing to emphasize the smallness of his wealth in proportion to someone of Simpson Lord's calibre.

"I'm glad you sold her," Dawn said because she felt some kind of response was necessary.

"A month after he bought her, the guy ran her into a reef," Slater informed her. "The *Seaspray* broke up and went to the bottom. But she didn't take your ghost with her."

Maybe it was the blandness in his announcement that made her suddenly so restless. Dawn really didn't know. "I'll go see if Randy needs any help," she murmured and moved away.

The boat's engines were kept a notch or two above idle speed until they had cleared the harbor, then Slater opened them up. The racing wind seemed to blow away Dawn's tension and allowed her to relax and enjoy the ride.

After Slater pointed out their destination on a nautical chart, she and Randy plotted a course to it. Each took a turn at the controls, and the hour it took to reach the spot on the map flashed by.

They anchored the cruiser in the deep water just off a coral reef and swam ashore. It only took Randy a few lessons to become accustomed to the use of the snorkeling equipment before he was initiated to the underwater beauty of a coral reef.

For Dawn, it was a matter of rediscovering all the little delights. It was a sport of wondrous beauty and serenity, the waters crystal clear and the colors of the fish and strange plant life displaying a rainbow brilliance. She was totally at peace—most of the time.

With a ten-year-old boy on the scene, there was bound to be some horseplay in the water. Usually it was between Randy and Slater but occasionally she was drawn into the playful fray. It just added to the fun of the afternoon.

All too soon it seemed, Slater was signaling them it was time to swim back to the boat. He was already on board when Dawn climbed the swimming ladder. Reaching down, he grabbed hold of her arm and hauled her onto the deck. Water streamed off of her as she looked up at him, smiling, a little out of breath from that last long swim, but blissfully contented.

His gaze glittered warmly onto her upturned face. "Enjoy yourself?"

"Yes," she breathed out the very definite answer. "I'd forgotten how wonderful it is out there."

She moved away so he could help Randy aboard. Exhausted but happy, she sank onto the aft deck, her legs curled to the side, and picked up a towel to towel-dry her hair. Randy was bubbling with enthusiasm over the adventure, talking nonstop from the second his feet touched the deck.

When he finally had to stop for a breath, Slater inserted, "It's late. If you two are going to get home in time for supper, we're going to have to get under way pretty soon."

"I'll help," Randy volunteered.

Dawn didn't even make an attempt to move,

except to straighten her legs out and lie back to let the sun evaporate the salt water from her skin. When she heard the fore and aft anchors being raised, she smiled and settled more comfortably on the hard deck. With two males on board, her help wasn't needed. She intended to simply lie there and soak up the sunshine.

The deck vibrated pleasantly with the purring throb of the engines. Her eyes were closed against the bright light of the sun. She was conscious of the boat's movement and the warmth of the sun on her skin, tempered by the coolness of an eddying wind. For a time she'd heard Slater and Randy conversing back and forth, but now there was only the sound of the boat and the splash of the water.

Something—a sixth sense maybe—seemed to warn her that she wasn't alone. She let her lashes raise just a crack and looked through the slitted opening. Slater was standing at her feet, silently looking at her. Her eyes opened a little wider.

A disturbing heat began to warm her blood. The way he was looking at her gave Dawn the uncanny feeling that in his mind, he was covering her. Without half-trying, she could feel the heat of his sun-warmed body against her skin and the pressure of his mouth on her lips, and the excitement building in her limbs.

It was a mental seduction, and all the more disturbing because of its intensity. It was like a spell being cast on her. Dawn knew she had to break it or it might cease to be mental.

She moved, shifting onto her side first to grab her beach jacket then rising to her feet. Without trying to make it seem deliberate, she turned her back to him while she turned out the jacket to locate the sleeves.

"Are we nearly there?" she asked to shatter the unbearable silence.

"About twenty minutes out."

His hands touched her waist, then slid around to the front to draw her backward against his length. Her heart did a funny little flip against her rib cage as one hand slid low on her stomach and the other curved to the underswell of her breasts. Spontaneous longing quivered through her. He bent his head and nibbled at her bare shoulder, adding to the effects the arousing caress of his hands created. Her fingers curled onto his forearms and weakly attempted to pull his hands away.

"You swore off drinking, Slater," Dawn reminded him in a voice that was all husky and disturbed.

"Yes, I swore off drinking," he admitted, his mouth moving near her ear, stimulating its sensitive shell-opening. "But there's no harm in caressing the bottle the wine comes in."

She turned into him, using her arms to wedge a space between them. "What will that accomplish?" Frustration flashed in the blue of her eyes as she discovered it was no less stimulating to feel her hips arched against his hard, male outline.

"I don't know." He locked his hands together in

122

the small of her back and eyed her lazily. "But you're going to ache almost as much as I will."

His mouth skimmed her face but didn't taste her intoxicating lips. She guessed he was testing his self-control and tried not to let him see that hers was stretched to the limit. When he finally drew away, she had the satisfaction of noting he was breathing no easier than she was. But there was also no question that he had aroused an ache that was slow to fade.

After they had docked the boat at the marina, they trooped to the car, none of them talking very much—not even Randy. He squeezed into the back of the Corvette and slumped tiredly.

"Boy, am I beat," he murmured.

"After working all morning and swimming all afternoon, you should be." Dawn knew she wasn't far away from exhaustion as she slid into the passenger seat. She was running on nerves, alert to every movement of Slater. "You'll have to get to bed early tonight," she told Randy. "It's work again in the morning."

"Don't listen to her, Randy," Slater advised and inserted the key in the ignition. "You don't have to work in the morning." Dawn opened her mouth to protest this usurption of her authority. Father or not, he had no right to countermand her orders without discussing it with her in private first. "Neither do you," he glanced at her, a small smile showing.

"I wasn't aware you had the authority to give me the day off," she replied a trifle stiffly.

"Let's just say that tomorrow you don't have to work in the yard," he said as if that avoided a confrontation.

"And why don't I?" Dawn challenged.

"Because while you two were getting cleaned up this noon, I took a crew of laborers over and had them finish the yard this afternoon."

"You had no right to do that!" Her stunned surprise was giving way to anger.

"Maybe I had no right to do it, but it's done," he stated. "If I had known you were going to try to clear that underbrush yourself, I would have done it to start out with—before you ever bought the house." He sliced her a short look. "I don't like the idea of either one of you handling all those sharp knives and blades. One careless mistake and you could cut yourself open to the bone."

"You could have discussed this with me first." She didn't argue against his logic, because she had been leery about Randy handling some of the sharper tools.

"I remember what it's like to argue with you when your mind's made up about something," Slater said dryly and shifted into reverse gear. "It's easier to have the discussion after the fact."

"I'm glad you hired those guys," Randy yawned from the back seat. "That was hard work."

"And it didn't hurt you a bit," Dawn flashed.

"I never said it did," Randy defended himself. "I'm just glad I don't have to do it again tomorrow morning."

"If you want to teach him work ethics, have him scrub floors or wash windows," Slater advised. "Going back to the basics is very noble, but there comes a point where it can be carried too far. A woman and a child clearing a jungle is taking it too far."

"So maybe it was," she admitted grudgingly, aware it had been a penny-pinching decision. "But since you took it upon yourself to hire those workmen, you can pay them, too."

"I planned on it." There was a trace of amusement in his voice. "You never did like letting go of your money, did you?"

"No." She turned her head to look out the side window, subsiding into silence.

Her mother looked around the front room with an approving nod. "It's looking so nice, Dawn."

"It's really beginning to look like a home, isn't it?" she said with satisfaction.

Half of their personal belongings had arrived by truck the same day Dawn received the deed to the house. The furniture and linen didn't arrive until the following week, and it took nearly the whole of another to get everything unpacked and organized.

In retrospect, it probably would have been best if she and Randy hadn't moved in until after everything was done. But Dawn had wanted them to be on their own, even if it meant living in the house while she was still trying to bring order to the chaos. Trying to juggle meals, dishwashing, bedmaking, and daily cleaning with the uncrating of boxes had only prolonged the day when it would all be done.

"And it's all going to look so much better when these drapes are hung," Dawn declared, walking over to the green and white sofa to pick up a freshly ironed panel. "They look beautiful, Mother."

"That material didn't turn out to be the easiest to sew, but I think they turned out rather well," she replied modestly.

The windows in the front room were odd-sized. After several fruitless shopping trips, Dawn had been finally forced to accept the drapes in the front room would have to be custom-made. She was spared the exorbitant price a decorator would have charged when her mother volunteered to make them.

"Those windows have been bare for so long." Dawn held the drape up, picturing the soft green color against the white walls. She looked at her mother and smiled. "Just imagine, I'll have privacy tonight. No one will be able to see in."

"Are you going to put them up tonight? Do you want me to stay and help you?" her mother offered.

"No, I can manage. You've done more than enough," Dawn insisted.

"If you're sure—" She didn't persist in her offer. "—I need to get home and start supper for your father. Randy's helping him in the garage. He's welcome to eat with us so you don't have to stop to fix him anything."

"No thanks." If she let her mother have her way, Randy would eat with them every night.

"It's time he learned he has to come home for supper."

"I'll send him home," her mother promised reluctantly and walked to the door. "Call if you need anything."

"I will."

Her mother's car hadn't left the driveway before Dawn was hauling the small stepladder into the living room so she could hang the pleated drapes at the windows. The two small side windows were a snap, but the large front window proved to be more of a hassle than she expected.

That area of the floor was warped, which meant the ladder wasn't balanced on all four legs so it rocked with each shift of her weight. Add to that, the drapes were wider by necessity and more awkward to handle because so much had to be held on her arm. She only had one hand free to fit the hook into its sliding eye-bracket, and to reach that she had to balance a knee on top of the ladder and stretch on tiptoe. It wasn't a position that promoted security. Dawn wished now that the ceilings that gave the house so much character weren't quite so high.

After much struggling, balancing, and stretching, she got one half of the front window set hung. There was still the other half to go. She moved the ladder over and observed how much it rocked. She debated waiting until Randy came home so he could hold the ladder steady, then decided to try it.

She tugged at the hem of her jean shorts and

gathered up the large panel, laying it over her arm. Her bare feet gripped the slatted steps of the ladder while it seesawed under her moving weight. Dawn took her time, testing the swaying rock of the ladder so she wouldn't accidentally overbalance the wrong way.

Then the slow process began of stretching and aiming for the eye, trying to hook it before it slid away and not losing her balance when the ladder rocked to a different three-point stance. It was nerve-wracking. When she heard footsteps crossing the veranda, Dawn sighed with relief.

As soon as the front door opened, she called, "Will you come over here and hold this ladder steady so I can finish hanging these drapes?"

She expected a grumble of protest from Randy, but none was voiced as she fumbled one-handed with the next hook to hold it in a position of readiness. When she felt a hand gripping the ladder, she made the final stretch for the bracket.

Suddenly there was a hand stroking the back of her thigh. Her eyes widened in shock at such familiarity from her son. She let go of the hook and swung her arm around to knock away his hand, turning to look at the same time.

"Randy!" His name was out of her mouth before Dawn saw Slater standing beside the ladder. "It's you!" She was almost relieved as her heart started beating again.

"I should hope it's me and not our son." There was something lazy and warm about the way he was looking at her. It did things to her pulse that still hadn't recovered from her initial start.

Since they had moved into the house, Slater had dropped by unannounced a couple of times, but Dawn had been expecting Randy and simply hadn't anticipated it might be anyone else. On his previous visits, Randy had always been at home. It was the first time they'd been alone since that night in his office.

"I didn't hear your car." Dawn noticed the way his dark hair gleamed with sun-burnished lights streaking through it. She wanted to reach down and smooth his unruly forelock the way she so often did Randy's.

"That's because I walked," Slater replied.

"If you're here to see Randy, he hasn't come home yet." Dawn turned back to the window and adjusted the drape material folded over her arm.

How many times had she seen Slater in the last two weeks? Easily more than a half a dozen times, sometimes on a matter related to the house and others when he'd come to see Randy. Even when the terms had been friendly, there had been a tension between them. It was difficult to be with him without wanting to touch and be closer.

"I suspected he wasn't." His voice was dry with amusement at her obvious announcement. Its tone altered when he added, "The drapes really make the room look different."

"They look good, don't they?" she said with smiling pride in the result, and grasped the hook she had dropped earlier to aim it for the eye bracket.

Just as she stretched for it, his hand trailed down the silken-smooth back of her leg. His touch went through her nerve ends like liquid lightning. She missed the bracket.

"Will you stop that?" she demanded.

"You have nice legs," Slater remarked with no remorse.

"Thank you." The compliment was almost as awkward to handle as his wayward hand.

His playful orneriness was unsettling. Her task was a difficult one requiring concentration and coordination. Slater was affecting both. She started to reach for the bracket again, then paused to look over her shoulder at him.

"Don't touch my leg. Okay?" she asked for his word, not liking the little silver light that danced in his charcoal-dark eyes.

"Okay," he agreed smoothly. Satisfied that he meant it, Dawn focused her gaze on the target and made her move for it. "You do have nice legs," Slater repeated. "Dirty feet, but nice legs." He ran a finger down the ticklish sole of her bare foot.

It was like testing her reflexes—all movement was involuntary. Her knee jerked, changing the center of her balance and tipping her forward. She yelped and grabbed for the top of the ladder to keep from going headfirst through the window.

The momentary fright had her heart beating like a racing motor. Her breath was coming in little gasps. It wasn't until her senses started quieting down that she felt his hand gripping the back pocket of her jean shorts. Obviously Slater had grabbed her to prevent her from pitching forward. But his efforts to save her weren't appreciated since he had been the cause in the first place.

She'd had to let go of everything. The unhung drape material was swinging drunkenly from the rod, attached to it by the first few hooks. She knew she wouldn't get the material folded so neatly again, which meant the material would be more cumbersome on her arm.

"Damn you, Slater MacBride," Dawn swore angrily. "You know the bottoms of my feet are ticklish."

"I think I'd forgotten *how* ticklish you are." There was a throaty chuckle in his voice. "Sorry. I won't do it again."

"You'd better not," she warned, unimpressed by his apology and its accompanying promise. "If you do that again, I'm liable to get myself killed."

"I certainly don't want that to happen," Slater murmured with an obvious effort to contain his amusement.

Dawn began hauling up the dangling portion of the drape panel and looping it over her arm. In her irritable mood, she didn't take as much care as she might have to keep the material from wrinkling.

"Will you just hold the ladder and keep your hands to yourself?" she demanded. "Don't touch me anywhere."

"I'll be as still as a mouse," he assured her.

Her first tries were tentative, not completely trusting him. Gradually, Dawn realized he intended to keep his word. The work went smoother after that.

When she had threaded the last hook through its eyes, she let her aching arms fall to her side and gazed with satisfaction at the smoothly hanging drapes with their crisp pleats spaced in neat rows. Not once had Slater intervened or even broken the silence. With the job done, she'd lost her irritation with him.

"They look great, don't they?" Dawn was eager to hear someone's opinion other than her own.

"Perfect," Slater agreed.

Unbending her knee, Dawn straightened her leg so her foot could find the ladder rung and join its twin. Her hands gripped the flat top of the ladder for balance so she could begin her descent.

With the first step, an arm hooked her legs and tugged her off balance so she was turning. A second arm circled her hips to finish the turn and lift her off the ladder. Her startled outcry was ignored and Dawn had to grab for his shoulders to keep from overbalancing.

Held high in the air by strong arms that hugged her hips to his chest, Dawn was helpless to do anything about it. She looked down at Slater's laughing features. The physical contact she'd longed for and the possessive gleam in his eyes made it impossible for her to even fake anger.

"Will you put me down?" There was a breathless catch in her voice.

"I don't think so." He was eye-level with her breasts that were angled away from him by her arched back, but he seemed quite fascinated by their nearness, and their movements under her cotton-thin blouse.

Dawn knew he was staring at them to disturb. It was confirmed when his glance flickered upward to measure her reaction. And there was one. Her lips were parted and her eyes were darkening with want. But she was too aware of recent bad experiences in his arms to give rein to her own desires.

"For a reformed alcoholic, you certainly play around with fire a lot." It was a husky accusation, a veiled attempt to remind him of his resolution concerning her.

His grip loosened, letting her slide down a few inches. "But there was a condition to my abstinence," Slater reminded her and nuzzled the blouse buttons that fastened the material across the valley between her breasts.

"What?" It was hard to think when sensation was trying to dominate her thought process.

His mouth shifted its area of interest to rub over the material covering the rounded sides of her breasts. "I said I'd stay away from you until I decided what I wanted." His murmuring voice was partially muffled by the cloth.

"And you decided?" Her eyes were closed and her head was bent toward him as her hands curled around his neck.

Slater eased her a little farther down to nuzzle the hollow of her throat, his lips and breath warm against her skin. "There was more agony doing without you, so I've decided to learn to live with my addiction."

She was lowered the last few inches until her toes touched the floor while he continued to nibble on her neck and to rub her jaw. Happiness soared through her at the news that he was bringing a close to his inner conflict.

"I thought you'd never make up your mind," she declared throatily.

"You don't know what it's been like for me since you came back," he asserted. "You're all I thought about. When I wasn't around you, I wanted to be. I dragged out closing the sale of the house just so I could have a legitimate reason to talk to you privately—away from Randy. I couldn't hold an intelligent conversation with anybody for more than five minutes without my mind wandering off with thoughts of you." His breath mingled with hers as his mouth became poised just above her lips. "It came down to a simple understanding. You're here—and I want you."

Her fingers tunneled into the thickness of his hair to force his head down. The union of their lips was a hungry testament of their need for each other that could not be culminated in a merely sexual act. Their bodies strained for more intimate contact, reaching wildly for the ultimate closeness that could never be adequately achieved.

As if coming from a great distance, there was the sound of running footsteps. The significance was lost on the entwined couple until the front door burst open and the intrusion startled them into breaking off the torrid kiss.

Chapter Eight

Randy halted abruptly, holding the door open and looking a little embarrassed as if he wasn't sure whether he should stay or go. Slater recovered first and withdrew his arms from around Dawn. Self-consciously, she smoothed the front of her blouse where it had ridden up.

"Grandma said I was to come home for supper," Randy said.

"Yes," Dawn nodded a little jerkily.

"I was just helping your mother off the stepladder," Slater explained.

Randy suddenly grinned and let go of the door, his light eyes glittering knowingly. "Next you'll be trying to convince me you two were practicing mouth-to-mouth resuscitation. I've been around, you know."

Slater laughed silently and glanced at Dawn. "Smart kid. Yours?"

"No, yours," she countered, smiling now, too.

"It's time the three of us had a discussion." He took her hand and drew her with him as he crossed to the sofa. Randy ambled over in the same direction and flopped in the armchair, eyeing them curiously.

"A discussion about what?" Dawn inquired into the subject matter as she settled onto a seat cushion beside Slater.

"I have a small problem, which I believe Randy shares," he said. She frowned slightly because the conversation wasn't taking the turn she expected. "We're father and son, but it's awkward for either of us to openly claim the relationship. We constantly would have to explain why his name is different from mine. It's probably more awkward for Randy because kids tend to call others names that can hurt."

A glance at Randy noted the tightness around his mouth, an admission that what Slater was saying was true. Dawn had known it was a potential problem, but she hadn't realized it had already surfaced.

"I've come up with a way to solve the problem," Slater announced.

"You have?" Randy gave him a wide-eyed look that was full of hope.

"Your mother and I can get married and have your name legally changed to mine." A faint satisfied smile curved his mouth as he explained his solution.

"That's great!" Randy declared, but Dawn kept her silence, stunned—not by his backhanded proposal—but his justification to Randy for their marriage. Then Randy laughed loudly. "When you do that, my name will legally be Randy MacBride MacBride. I'll be a MacBride twice."

"I guess you will." Slater smiled along with him.

Dawn finally found her voice. "I thought this was supposed to be a discussion between the three of us. It sounds like the two of you have made a decision without even asking my opinion," she pointed out. "It is going to affect me."

"I wanted to hear what Randy thought of my solution before I asked you about it—privately," he stressed the latter, an engaging smile deepening the corners of his mouth.

"Randy—" she turned to her son, struggling to keep calm until she found out what Slater had to say, "—why don't you go get cleaned up for supper."

This was a discussion she didn't want postponed. She needed her suspicions put to rest, and soon, or they'd eat away at her.

"Okay." He pushed out of the chair and paused. "You know you think it's a good idea, too."

"Go," she urged without denying his statement.

Her gaze followed him as he left the room and lunged up the stairs, taking the steps two at a time. She waited until she heard him in the upstairs bathroom before she glanced at Slater.

"Did you mean that about getting married?" she asked, with a searching look.

"Like Randy said, it's a good idea," he repeated while his fingers curled tighter around her hand.

"It's never any good for two people to get married for the sake of a child," she insisted, wanting him to give her a better reason than that. "It wouldn't be any good for us, either, even if it makes the situation easier for Randy."

"It'll be good." He slipped an arm around her waist and pulled at her hand to draw her closer to him.

Her free hand pushed at his shoulder to keep from being drawn into his embrace while she turned her face away from his descending mouth. "I have to know why you want to marry me—whether it's only because of Randy." She wouldn't be persuaded into accepting by his kisses.

When she drew her head back to look at him, Slater sighed heavily and didn't try to pursue his quarry. "Don't you know?" There was a half-teasing light in his eyes. "Maybe I want to marry you for your money?"

Dawn went white. "If that's supposed to be a joke, I don't think it's very funny."

"I don't suppose it is," he agreed, the light fading. "It would be poetic justice, wouldn't it? This would be my first time at the marriage altar, so I should be wedding money—according to you."

Hurt that he would continue with this terrible joke—if it was a joke—Dawn tried to twist her hand out of his grasp and pull it free. Slater just laughed in his throat and gathered her into his arms.

"You didn't think I was serious?" He rebuked her for questioning his motive while his gaze burned possessively over her features. "I thought I'd made it plain before Randy ever walked in the

138

door how I felt about you." His lips brushed her cheek in a gentle and reassuring caress.

"It was cruel to tease me like that." There was a hint of desperation in the way her arms went around him to cling. If it hadn't been for her own guilty conscience about the way she had treated him long ago, she probably would have laughed off his joking suggestion. "I'm too sensitive, I guess."

"It was a foolish way for me to let you know that I was putting all that kind of thinking behind us." Slater took part of the blame. "But it's something we both have to tread lightly around, it seems."

Dawn suspected he was right. There were too many years of hurt that couldn't be wiped out with the wave of any magic wand—even love. But understanding that would carry them a long way in overcoming it.

"I'm still curious about something." She reluctantly drew back so she could see his face, but this time made no attempt to expand the circle of his arms.

"What's that?" He playfully kissed the tip of her nose.

"Why did you allow Randy to think we were getting married because of him?" she asked.

"Because I wanted him to see how our marriage would benefit him, then gradually ease him into discovering that he was going to have to share a lot of your time with me." A sudden smile flashed across his features. "And I wanted him on my side just in case you got stubborn and thought we should wait awhile before tying the knot."

"Trying to gang up on me, were you?" Dawn accused with a provocative look through the tops of her lashes.

"That's one of the benefits of having a son. We'll always have you outnumbered," he warned. "Speaking of numbers, I have something to give you."

Releasing her, he stretched out a leg and reached inside his pants pocket. She caught a gleam of shiny metal as he reached for her left hand.

"Numbers equals digits equals fingers," Slater explained his word association and slipped an engagement ring on her finger. "A sapphire—to match your eyes."

"It's beautiful." Dawn stared at it, adequate words escaping her, but the brilliant shimmer in her blue eyes rivaled the deep color of the sparkling stone when she finally looked at him.

"I remembered that Simpson had given you a diamond and I didn't want to follow in his footsteps," he admitted.

Dawn wished he hadn't mentioned him. It tarnished some of the joy in the moment, but she couldn't block the memory of him out of her life. It was time both of them began treating his name as belonging to a mutual acquaintance.

"He always followed in yours," Dawn corrected him.

"I'm glad you quit wearing his rings," he said.

Before she could explain that she had sold them, Randy chose that moment to clump loudly down the steps. He halted on the last one and called, "Is it safe to come down?" This time he gave them forewarning before bursting into the room.

"It's safe," Slater chuckled.

He bounded jauntily into the room, his gaze darting from one to the other. "Well? What did she say?"

"Take a look." Slater lifted her left hand for Randy's inspection of the engagement ring.

"Great! Now that we've got that out of the way, what's for supper?" His hunger took precedence over any prolonged celebration of their engagement.

The abrupt change of subject startled a laugh from her. "Oh, Randy," she declared in amusement.

"Well?" The challenging inflection of his voice made it a defensive word. "You told me to get cleaned up for supper, so what are we going to eat—and when? I'm starving."

"You're always starving," Dawn insisted with an indulgent look.

"He takes after me," Slater murmured and bit at the lobe of her ear. "I'm hungry, too." But the growling sound of his voice spoke of an appetite that had nothing to do with food.

A response to that was impossible with Randy listening in, so Dawn attempted to deal with her son first. "I haven't started anything for supper so you have your choice of hamburger—or hamburger."

"That's a lot of choice," Slater laughed. "How are we supposed to make up our minds?"

"Let's have hamburgers," she suggested with a laugh.

"How long's it going to take?" Randy asked.

"If I had two handsome helpers, I bet supper would be on the table in half an hour. How hungry are you?" Dawn challenged.

It looked as if Randy's appetite was fading, but Slater rolled to his feet and clamped a hand on the boy's shoulder. "You've got your two volunteers."

She stood up. "The kitchen is that way." She pointed to the hallway behind them. Slater turned Randy around and marched him toward it while Dawn brought up the rear.

"What do you want us to do?" Slater asked.

"Randy can set the table and you—" she opened the refrigerator and tossed him the packet of hamburger, "—can grill the hamburgers."

"What are you going to do?" Randy protested what he saw as an unfair division of labor.

"I'm going to put the frozen french fries in the oven and make a salad," she said and took a head of lettuce out of the refrigerator's vegetable bin.

Slater exchanged a glance with Randy. "She's a regular general handing out orders." He slid her a look as he formed the hamburger into patties. "Do I have your permission to wear the pants in our family?"

Pausing by the stove where Slater was working, Dawn turned the oven on to heat. Her arm brushed slightly against his, attracting his downward sideglance.

"You can wear the pants." She saucily gave him permission.

142

Before she could elude the retaliation she expected, he hooked an arm around her waist and hugged her to his side. He bent his head near her ear. She tipped her cheek up to him, expecting a kiss.

Instead, Slater murmured, for her hearing alone, "I don't care who wears the pants as long as neither one of us wears them to bed." As he let his hand fall from her waist, he playfully pinched her bottom.

"Ouch!" But she was laughing as she quickly backed away from him.

"Hey, I've been wondering." Randy frowned as he circled the table, dispensing plates at the three place settings. "Where are we going to live after you two get married?"

Dawn had been riding so high on her newfound happiness that she hadn't thought about such details. "The house, we just bought it." She hated the idea of moving out of it when they had barely settled in.

"Considering that I have only a one-bedroom apartment, I think we would all be more comfortable if I moved in here." Slater eliminated her concern.

"Well, when are you going to get married?" Randy asked.

"As soon as possible." Both answered the question simultaneously, then looked at each other and laughed at their mutual haste.

"We'll probably get married the end of the week," Slater was more specific. "I should be able to arrange to get away from the business for a couple of days. That, combined with the weekend, should enable us to take a short honeymoon." He looked at Dawn, silently seeking her approval of his plan. "I thought we could go away on my boat."

"I'd like that," she nodded, her face beaming with a smile because they had once spent so much of their time together on his old boat.

"Can I come, too?" Randy thought it sounded like fun.

"Absolutely not," Slater laughed. "The three of us will go out for a weekend *after* your mother and I have our honeymoon. How's that?"

"Since I don't have any choice, I guess it has to be okay," he declared with a dismal shrug of his shoulders. "The table's all set. I'm done."

"I don't see the salt and pepper," Dawn noticed. "What about ketchup and mustard? All those things are part of setting the table."

"Aw, Mom," Randy grumbled, but added the missing items to the table.

Less than half an hour after the three of them converged on the kitchen, they were sitting down to the meal. When Randy reached for his third hamburger, Slater eyed him skeptically then glanced at Dawn.

"Does he always eat like that or haven't you fed him the last couple of days?" he asked, more to tease Randy than anything else.

She just smiled. "Wait until you find out how expensive it is to feed a growing boy." Once that hadn't been of any concern to her until she had to start managing on a limited budget. With the food on her plate gone, Dawn stood up to carry it to the sink. "Coffee?"

"Sounds good," Slater nodded.

"Do I have to help with dishes?" Randy wanted to know.

"Not tonight," Dawn told him as she set her plate in the sink and took down two cups from the cupboard.

"Then is it all right if I go over to Gramps'?" he asked, already pushing his chair back from the table. "We're making a table."

"What about your hamburger?" Slater glanced at the sandwich Randy had just taken with only one bite gone from it.

"Oh, I'll eat it on the way," he said, unconcerned.

"You can go," Dawn excused him from the table. He grabbed up the sandwich and bolted for the door. "Don't forget to be home before dark!" she called after him. There was a wry shake of her head as she carried the filled coffee cups to the table. "He eats and never stops; he runs and never walks."

"All I can say is—" Slater waited until she had set the cups on the table, then grabbed her hand and pulled her onto his lap, "—alone at last."

"I thought you wanted coffee." She linked her hands behind his neck and settled comfortably against his chest. Her finger felt pleasantly heavy with the weight of her engagement ring.

"To tell you the truth—" he ran his hand up her thigh and over her hip to her waist, "—that isn't what I'm thirsty for."

The driving pressure of his kiss drank deeply from her lips. It ignited a ground swell of desire that flamed through her veins. The completeness of her love was almost shattering to behold. The heat surged through her limbs, melting bones and flesh. His roaming hand cupped itself to the underswell of her breast, his thumb stroking the tip in heady stimulation, her thin blouse holding back none of the delicious sensations.

With a bang of the screen door, Randy charged into the house and came to a sliding stop. "Whoops!" His ears reddened at the sight of them.

"I thought you went to your grandparents'," Slater said with a trace of exasperation, but continued to hold Dawn on his lap.

"I did—I am," Randy was flustered. "I just came back to see if it was all right for me to tell them that you're getting married."

"Of course, you can tell them," Dawn replied.

"Okay." His mouth twitched in a hesitant smile as he backed to the door. "Bye."

When the door had closed, Slater studied her wryly. "You know what's going to happen in about ten minutes, don't you?"

"What's that?" She smoothed her hand over the slanting line of his jaw.

"Your mother is either going to call or come over so she can be the first to congratulate us."

"You're probably right." Her mouth lifted in a crooked smile. "Pop will probably come over, too."

"Which means they won't leave until dark," Slater concluded. "What's Randy's bedtime?"

"Eleven o'clock."

An exaggerated groan came from his throat before he smothered it by kissing her fiercely. She felt his frustration and echoed it with her own. They'd been apart so long that he was impatient with anything that kept them apart any longer.

His tongue licked at her lips, sensuously going over their outline, then threading its way between them. She was filled with the taste of him, so heady and male. The buttons of her blouse were unfastened one by one, and his invading hand pushed the material aside to explore the bared flesh. There was an involuntary tightening of her stomach muscles at the touch of his hand.

A storm shower of kisses moistly covered her face, closing her eyes while Dawn trembled in the throes of growing passion. It stopped so Slater could view the prize he held in his lap. Through the slits of her lashes, she saw the pleased look in his heavily lidded eyes and took pleasure in her womanly shape.

Her back was arched slightly by the pressure of his arm as he bent his head to kiss the pouting tip of a breast, briefly taking it between his teeth and tracing its hardness with his tongue. Her hands tightened around his neck in instant reaction. A half-satisfied smile played with the corners of his mouth as he turned away to rub his cheek against hers, his breath stirring the hair near her ear.

"Are you sure you don't want to change your mind about getting married on Friday?" he murmured against her skin. "The ceremony isn't going to be up to your standards, you know."

"What do you mean?" Dawn was too bemused by his kisses and caressing hands to devote her whole attention to what he was saying.

Talk seemed unnecessary at a time like this. Of course, that wasn't all he was doing. His hands continued their roaming ways, stroking thigh and hipbone, sensually rubbing and familiarizing themselves with the shape of her.

"There won't be time to make it a lavish affair with hundreds of guests. The wedding party will consist of you and me—and your parents, I suppose, as our witnesses. You'll be lucky to find a wedding dress, let alone a trousseau. There won't be tons of wedding gifts to open, nor a grand reception." Slater continued rubbing his mouth over her cheek, not letting the conversation interfere with his loveplay. "Just a quickie marriage."

"It sounds perfect." She didn't need to tell him that she'd been through all that. "I've become very fond of simple things."

"Meaning me?" He took a tenderly punishing bite of her ear in revenge and Dawn wiggled at the peculiar blend of exquisite pleasure and pain his love-nip induced.

"You're far from simple," she insisted huskily. "As a matter of fact, I think you're very complicated. It's going to take me the rest of my life to figure you out."

"Just so long as you remember it is for the rest of your life," Slater murmured and rolled his mouth across her lips in a sealing kiss.

"I do." Dawn lovingly trailed a finger over his tanned cheekbone down to his mouth, running it over its masculine firmness. "At this moment, Friday seems far away. But I know it's going to be hectic getting the blood tests, applying for the license and arranging for a minister, not to mention finishing all the things I have to do here in the house—and moving your things in."

"And me," he added.

"And moving you in, too," she smiled.

"You can always hire someone to do it for you instead of trying to do all this housework, unpacking, and moving yourself," Slater pointed out.

"But I like doing it myself," Dawn insisted.

"Right now it's all a novelty to you, but you'll get tired of it," he predicted. Then his expression grew serious, his gaze narrowing to bore deeply. "What happens when the newness wears off, Dawn? You're used to the excitement of big city life. What happens when this life become too tame and boring?"

"It won't happen." She didn't even have to think about her answer.

She was very positive about it because she had experienced both kinds of life and knew the advantages and disadvantages of both. Now she knew precisely what she wanted.

"It better not." His arms tightened around her, crushing her to his ribs while he roughly kissed her lips.

The roughness fled quickly as desire took hold and made it a moistly heated exchange. Her position in his lap became a dissatisfying one, too passive when she wanted to be an active participant in this embrace.

"Dawn!!" The sound of her name ended on a high, questioning note. She instantly recognized the voice as belonging to her mother, and she was calling from the living room. Neither had heard the front door open.

Quickly she catapulted herself off of Slater's lap and began buttoning her blouse. "It's mother," she hissed needlessly, trying to put her clothes into some kind of order before she responded to the calling voice.

"So much for being alone," he murmured dryly, and watched her frantic efforts with a trace of amusement. "It lasted just long enough for us to get hot and bothered—and not long enough to do anything about it."

She flashed him a glance that held both amusement and a trace of embarrassment at his frank assessment. Another call came from the living room, and Dawn couldn't delay answering any longer.

"We're in the kitchen, Mother!" she called, and grabbed up some dishes to carry them to the sink. She threw a glance over her shoulder at Slater, still seated in the chair. "Aren't you going to help?"

"I think it's best if I stay seated," he replied and chuckled at the faint blush that tinted her cheeks.

"Randy just told us the news." Her mother started talking excitedly before she even walked into the kitchen. She beamed at both of them. "I'm so happy for you. Randy said the wedding was going to be Friday and I just knew that couldn't be right, so I came over—"

"It's going to be Friday," Dawn inserted.

"But there's so much to do beforehand," her mother protested.

"Not really. It's going to be a very simple ceremony—with just you and Pops—and Randy, of course," she explained as she carried a cup of coffee to the table for her mother.

"Even at that, there's still things to be done." A little agitated, she sat down and began listing them, ticking them off her fingers as she thought of them. "An announcement has to be placed in the paper. And flowers to be ordered. Even if you don't carry a bouquet, you'll at least want a corsage. And a wedding cake; you'll want a small one if nothing else."

"Just a small one," Dawn conceded, caught up in the snowball.

"And as for the reception afterward—" her mother began.

"We'll have drinks on my boat after the ceremony," Slater interrupted.

"And what will you wear? You'll want to buy a new dress," her mother continued. "And Randy—he's outgrowing all his clothes."

Turning his head, Slater glanced at Dawn. "What was that you said about 'simple'?" he mocked the growing length of the list.

Chapter Nine

In sleep, Dawn lay on her stomach with her cheek burrowed into the pillow. Her hand felt its way across the bunk's mattress to locate Slater, but the space beside her was empty. The information registered in her subconscious, prodding her awake.

Frowning sleepily, she turned her head and looked at the hollowed-out place where Slater had been sleeping. His head had left an impression in the pillow and the musky smell of him clung to the sheets.

Sunshine came through the portals, finishing the rousing process; Dawn rolled onto her back and pushed the copper hair away from her face as she listened intently for some sound of Slater moving about on the boat. When she heard his tuneless whistle, she smiled and pulled the light cover up, tucking it under her arms, conscious of the pleasantly rough sensation of cotton sheets against her naked skin.

A languid contentment seemed to have taken all the strength from her muscles, as well as any inclination to leave the bed where she had enjoyed so much loving last night. Her smile deepened at the satisfying memory of it. Just thinking about it produced a little quiver of excitement.

She hugged the cover more tightly across her breasts and glanced at the gold wedding band that had joined the sapphire engagement ring on her finger. "Mrs. MacBride," Dawn murmured, liking the sound of it and feeling like a giddy schoolgirl for trying it out.

Since Slater dominated the subject of her thoughts, her curiosity naturally ran to what he was doing. She could hear him whistling, but there wasn't any sound of him moving about on deck. But there were odd thumps and clunks, and a soft scraping sound that puzzled her.

Between the wondering and the desire to be with him, she tossed back the light cover and swung out of the wide bunk. His white terry-cloth robe hung on a hook. Dawn hesitated, then slipped it on and tied the swaddling bulk around her. She glanced at her reflection in the oval mirror. The provocative gleam that entered her blue eyes indicated a satisfaction with the resulting look.

As she passed through the small galley, she noticed the pot of coffee on the stove and an empty cup sitting on the counter beside it. She stopped and poured a cup for Slater and one for herself before proceeding up the hatchway to the deck. Trying to keep an eye on the cups, she glanced around to locate Slater.

"Good morning?" She didn't see him. "How about some coffee?" She wrinkled her nose as she caught the acrid smell of marine enamel.

"Good morning," Slater answered.

When she glanced in the direction of his voice, Dawn saw him hanging over the side of the boat, secured by some sort of rope swing. She frowned curiously and started across the deck to see what he was doing. At the moment, all she could see was his head and the top part of his bare chest.

"What are you doing?" The paint smell grew stronger as she approached. "Is this any way to spend your honeymoon? Painting a boat?"

"You get away from here." He motioned her backward with a wave of his paintbrush. "This is supposed to be a surprise, so you can't look yet. I'll be through in a minute."

"A surprise?" Dawn halted, then took a couple of steps sideways to sit in a deck chair. "What are you doing?"

"What does it look like I'm doing?" Slater countered with a smug little smile.

She was aware of his concentration, and the almost painstaking strokes he seemed to be making. "It looks like you're writing something." Her eyes widened at the conclusion that followed that. "Are you changing the name of the boat?"

"Clever girl," he smiled.

A little thrill went through her, guessing that he must be naming it after her if it was supposed to be a surprise. "What if *Homesick* doesn't like it?" she said, giving the boat an identity.

"She'll have to like it," Slater replied, "She doesn't have any choice."

"Your coffee is going to get cold if you don't hurry," she warned, nearly eaten up with curiosity herself.

He didn't answer immediately as he concentrated on the last bit of lettering. Then a smile was breaking across his face. "All done." He looked at her for an instant, then shifted his position to haul himself on board.

An invitation wasn't required as Dawn set the coffee cups on the deck and hurried to the side. Slater was clad only in a pair of cutoff jeans, the legs frayed to form a rough fringe. His outstretched arm checked her haste.

"Careful," he advised. "You don't want to get any wet paint on you."

His word of caution prompted her to look where she was putting her hands before she leaned forward to peer over the side. It took her a minute to read the lettering upside-down. There was a sudden rush of tears as she straightened and turned to Slater.

"The Second Time." Her voice choked on a bubble of emotion. "Oh, Slater." Her chin quivered and she tried to laugh at her overly sentimental response.

"It is the second time—for us—and being together on a boat," He quietly reinforced his choice with an explanation, and reached for her left hand, rolling his thumb across her wedding rings. "Only this time, it's my ring you're wearing in the morning."

She wrapped her arms around his bare middle and hugged him close, resting her cheek against his flatly muscled chest and closing her eyes. "Thank you for *The Second Time*. It's a wonderful wedding present for both of us."

He tucked a hand under her chin and lifted it to kiss her mouth, with long, drugging warmth. When he finally raised his head, it was to lazily study her upturned face.

"I suppose you know how sexy you look in my robe," he murmured and let his gaze trail downward to the gaping front and the exposed swell of her breasts.

Dawn started to deny any foreknowledge, then grinned saucily. "Yes."

"Brazen hussy," he accused mockingly and kissed her hard, then let her go. "I'll have that cup of coffee now."

"Tease," she accused, but let him take her by the hand and lead her back to the deck chair, where he pulled one alongside of hers.

After they were seated with their respective cups in hand, their fingers stayed linked in loving companionship. All around them was stillness, the quiet lapping of water against the boat's hull interrupted only by the distant cry of a bird.

The boat was anchored inside the entrance to a small sheltered cove of an uninhabited key away from the more frequently traveled water routes. Slater had sailed to it last night, so Dawn had seen little of it in the dark.

With a midmorning sun shining on its sandy

shore, she was taking her first good look at it. It seemed a tropical paradise with its blue waters and swaying palms. Although it appeared uninhabited at first glance, Dawn revised that opinion as she began noticing the variety of birds—long-legged herons, squatty white pelicans, and a roseate spoonbill, as well as a circling osprey.

"No wonder Audubon spent so much time in the Keys," she murmured. "It's teeming with exotic birdlife." Turning her head, she glanced at Slater. "Why don't we spend our honeymoon here instead of hopping around to other places? It's so beautiful and peaceful."

"We can." He drained his coffee cup and set it on the deck. "Want to go for a swim before breakfast?"

"Sure." She started to stand up. "Just give me a minute to change into my swimsuit."

His fingers tightened their link with hers. "Why bother?" he challenged. "We've got the place all to ourselves so why not swim in the nude?"

"Why not? I will if you will," she said with a little shrug and stood up. "Deal?"

"It's a deal," he agreed, but he was suspicious of the little gleam in her eyes.

"I'll race you to the beach," Dawn challenged. "Last one there has to cook breakfast."

With a quick tug of the sash, the robe fell open and Dawn slipped out of it. Slater was still unzipping his cutoffs when she dove over the side and struck out for shore. The time it took him to strip was the handicap she needed. Even though she was a strong swimmer, she was no match for Slater.

Even with the headstart, he nearly caught up with her. She waded onto the sand only two steps ahead of him. Breathless from the exertion, she collapsed onto the smooth sand and lay back on her elbows. Her blue eyes were sparkling with triumphant laughter that she didn't have the wind to voice.

"You have to cook . . . breakfast," she informed him between gulps for air.

"You cheated." He dropped onto the sand beside her, breathing hard, water dripping from him.

"Now why should you complain because I can undress faster than you?" Dawn blinked her eyes at him with mock innocence. "I should think a man would be overjoyed about that."

"You think so, eh?" Slater shifted to lean over her in a threatening posture.

But the leap of awareness in her senses was not caused by alarm. She lifted her chin to gladly take the kiss he pressed onto her mouth. The weight of his chest collapsed the support of her elbows, sinking her slowly backward on the sand, the wet, warmth length of his body stretching out alongside hers.

Her arms curved around him, a hand exploring the sinewed ridges of his backbone. When he dragged his mouth away, his gaze burned a look over her face and chest. She ran the tip of her tongue across her lips.

"You taste like salt," she identified the briny substance that had moistened his kiss.

"So do you," he murmured. "But I always did like the taste of salt on my food." As if to prove it, he began to show her how much he enjoyed her salty flavor.

It was an idyllic time, hours lazily drifting into one another. They swam, fished, tramped the island, snorkeled, sun-bathed, and made love. If it weren't for the nightly ship-to-shore calls they made to talk to Randy and for Slater to check with his office, it was as if they were isolated from the rest of the world.

In a bulky gray sweatshirt and a headband keeping the copper-red hair off her neck, Dawn gazed at the tranquil cove. A late afternoon sun had created a new pattern of shadows, which she studied, intent on memorizing the way it looked.

A pair of arms stole around her waist, but she knew their feel. Her hands gripped them and helped them to tighten their circle while she tipped her head to the side and give Slater free access to the curve of her neck.

"Mmm, delicious," he murmured, nibbling on it. "Unfortunately—" he sighed, "—it doesn't take the place of food. Let's have an early dinner."

Dawn carried his suggestion one step further. "Let's build a fire on the beach and have a cookout."

There was a short silence while he considered her suggestion. "Why not," he agreed. "Get the stuff together so we can load it into the rubber dinghy."

After they got the food and utensils ashore, Slater gathered driftwood and built a fire while Dawn wrapped the potatoes, vegetables, and yellowtail fish in individual foil packets for roasting on the coals. The meal was ready in time for them to eat by the light of a lingering sun. Then they settled back with a cup of campfire coffee to watch the orange ball of flame sink into the ocean. The sunset splashed the sky with corals and pinks and lavenders.

A breeze stirred to life with the setting of the sun, cool as it came off the waters. The warmth from the flickering fire was just enough to ward off any chill. Dawn leaned back in Slater's arms and used his chest for a pillow while she waited for the moonrise to silver the cove.

"That sunset was specially ordered," Slater said, his breath stirring her hair as he tipped his head slightly down. "Did you like it?"

"It was beautiful," she assured him, although by now her mind had begun wandering down another path, one far from the island. "How much do you think it would cost to lease one of those shops in Old Town?"

"I don't know." He sounded amused by her question from left field. "I imagine it would depend on a lot of things—the square footage of floor space, location, the condition of the building. Why?"

"I've been thinking about leasing some space, and opening a shop. My father makes some beautiful things and I know they would sell if they were marketed right. Heaven knows, he has enough inventory in his garage to stock the place," she added wryly.

Slater shifted to the side in order to better see her face. "I'm surprised. I always thought your father was too proud and stubborn to let someone else—even his daughter—provide the financing to set him up in business."

"I wasn't thinking of setting him up in business. I thought I'd operate the shop. Maybe my mother could work part-time in it." She considered that possibility. "That way both of them would be earning some extra money to supplement their pension."

"Why would you want to operate the shop?" There was a frown in his voice.

"Don't tell me you're one of those husbands who believes a wife's place is at home?" Dawn teased.

"The idea isn't totally unpleasant," he admitted dryly. "But that doesn't answer my question."

"It's very simple. I want to earn some money. No woman wants to ask her husband for every penny of her spending money," she defended her stand.

He chuckled in vague confusion, his chest moving under her head. "You're worried about asking me for spending money?" He was amused by the thought. "What about the Lord family fortunes? There must be a moldy dollar or two lying around, doing nothing."

She laughed, suddenly understanding why he was puzzled. "I forgot to tell you. Simpson didn't leave me anything when he died. Oh, he did arrange for me to receive a yearly living allowance, but that stopped when I married you."

"What?" It was a low, surprised question.

"It's true," she assured him. "I was told I could contest the will since I was legally his wife and I hadn't signed any marriage contract that negated my claim to his estate. But it just didn't seem to matter anymore."

"Where did you get the money for the house?" he asked in that same slightly disbelieving voice.

"I sold all the jewelry Simpson had given me. He also set up a trust fund for Randy's college education," Dawn added. "So, at least, we won't have to worry about that expense."

"No."

A pale, fatly shaped crescent moon rested above the horizon. "Look, there's the moon." She called Slater's attention to it. "It's beautiful, isn't it?"

"Yes."

She snuggled into his arms and pulled them more tightly around her waist. "It's too bad we can't stay here forever," she sighed.

"You can't have everything, Dawn." He unwrapped his arms from around her and gripped her shoulders to sit her up. "It's time we were getting the dinghy loaded and headed back for the boat."

"So soon?" she protested and stayed curled or

the sand while Slater rolled to his feet and kicked out the fire.

"Yes, so soon."

"Spoilsport," she accused and held out her hand so he could pull her up.

There was a split-second hesitation before he grasped it and hauled her to her feet. But it didn't flow into an embrace as she thought it might. Instead Slater walked over and picked up the basket loaded with dirty dishes and gear.

"It is early." Dawn shook out the blanket and began to fold it.

"It will be early in the morning when we leave, too," he replied.

"Leave?" She stared at him. "To go where?"

"Back to Key West." His features were in shadow, the pale moon not providing sufficient light to let her see his expression.

"But I thought we didn't have to go back for another two days," she frowned and trailed after him when he headed for the dinghy, grounded on the beach a few yards away.

"Something's come up and I'm needed back at the office." It was a very uncommunicative answer.

"But—when you talked to Mrs. Greenstone this afternoon—afterward you said everything was running smoothly." Dawn was positive he hadn't mentioned there were any problems.

"Dawn—" he stopped and turned to look at her, the utmost of patience in his tone, "—things can be running smoothly, but there still can be an item that requires my personal attention. There wasn't any reason to mention it earlier, because I didn't want to spoil your last evening."

"Well, it's spoiled," she declared, but mainly by his attitude.

"You knew we had to go back sometime," he stated.

"Of course, I did. I'm not a child," she retorted, a little snappishly. "And you didn't have to keep it from me as if I were a child."

"Have it your way," Slater muttered and turned away to stow the basket in the dinghy.

It was a short, and very silent, ride back to the boat. Dawn glanced at the name gleaming on the white hull—*The Second Time*. It had a bitter ring to it somehow.

In the same tense silence, they unpacked the dishes and utensils from the cookout. When Slater went up on deck, Dawn went into the head and used the shower. The cleansing spray seemed to drive out her moody resentment. By the time she had toweled dry, she was regretting her participation in this silent war. She didn't want their last evening to come to a close on such a sour note.

Hoping it would spark a more pleasant memory, she grabbed his terrycloth robe and tied it around her. As she started down the narrow companionway, she noticed Slater sitting at the table in the galley. A briefcase sat on the bench beside him. A folder of papers was opened on the table while he worked a pocket calculator and made notes on a yellow tablet.

"Aren't you coming to bed?" She paused in the opening to the galley, a bare foot resting on the raised threshold.

He didn't even look up at her question. "No. I have to go over these papers before tomorrow."

"In that case, I'll put on some coffee and sit up with you." Dawn started to enter the galley.

"No. Go on to bed." He refused her offer with disinterest. "You know I can concentrate better when you're not around."

She should have felt complimented by that, but he hadn't even looked at her once. He was trying to claim she was a distraction, yet his concentration hadn't faltered once. His fingers continued to tap out numbers on the calculator.

But there didn't seem to be any point on which she could argue. "Good night," she said.

"Good night." His attention remained on his work, his response absently given.

Alone, she climbed into bed and stared at the ceiling, waiting for him to join her. Her mind went back over the evening, trying to pinpoint just when it had gone wrong. It was just shortly after she had told Slater that she was not the rich widow he thought her to be. She had called his attention to the rising moon; then he had said it was time to leave. It had all gone downhill after that.

Had he sounded upset that she wasn't rich? The minute her mind asked the question, Dawn shook it away. Knowing Slater's pride, he was probably relieved that she didn't have another man's money. Besides, he had just been joking when he'd said he was marrying her for her money. It was absurd to think such a thing—and worse to take it seriously, even for a minute.

It was possible he'd been upset because she'd kept it from him. He could have felt she should have confided in him before. But it was no more than that. Dawn rolled onto her side and glanced at the reflected light from the galley. Her eyelids drifted down as she wondered how late he would work.

When she wakened the next morning, it was to the throb of the engines. She sat up, rubbing the sleep from her eyes and holding on to the edge of the bunk to combat the boat's motion. Although she couldn't remember hearing Slater come to bed, the covers were all rumpled on his side.

Since they were already underway, she couldn't delay their departure by lingering in bed. Dawn pushed aside the covers and climbed out to wash quickly and dress.

The skyline of Key West was an indistinct blur on the horizon when she joined Slater at the bridge. "Why didn't you wake me?" she asked, raising her voice to make herself heard above the engines.

"No point." He shrugged, dragging his gaze from the water long enough to aim it in her general direction.

A swirling wind whipped her hair across her face. She turned into it so it would blow it back. The idyllic days seemed to be gone and they were rushing back into the world where it wasn't all love and tranquility.

"I guess the honeymoon's over," Dawn said, but she didn't think it had been loud enough for Slater to hear. She was wrong.

"Nothing lasts forever," he stated.

Maybe that was it, she decided as buildings began to take shape on the horizon. Maybe things had been too perfect, and she had been foolishly expecting them to stay that way. Maybe, last night, both of them had been resenting it couldn't always be as sublime as it had been in that tropical cove.

An hour later they had docked and loaded their suitcases in the trunk of the Corvette. Slater helped her into the passenger seat, then walked around to slide behind the wheel. He still seemed preoccupied and withdrawn, even when he looked at her.

"Where do you want me to drop you off?" He inserted the key in the ignition and started the motor. "At home or your parents'?"

For a stunned second, Dawn couldn't answer. "Aren't you coming home?"

"No." His patience seemed worn. "I told you I had business to handle. I'm going to drop you wherever you want to go and head straight for the office."

"I know that's what you said." There was a hint of sharpness in her answer.

"Well?" Slater prodded. "Which is it?"

"Take me home." It was amazing how he could whip an answer out of her when she wanted to burn him with her silence.

The Corvette seemed to speed through the

streets, not slackening its pace until it swung in the driveway of the "Conch-style" house. While Dawn dug the key out of her purse, Slater lifted the suitcases out of the trunk and set them by the sidewalk. When he slid behind the wheel and shut the door, Dawn stared at him in a kind of angry shock.

"Aren't you even coming in?" she demanded.

"No." He glanced at the suitcases sitting by the walk. "They aren't heavy. You should be able to manage them."

It wasn't the suitcases she had been thinking about. This was their new home. She thought he might carry her over the threshold, but she wasn't about to mention it and possibly have him laugh at her for being so foolishly romantic.

The honeymoon was over in spades.

Chapter Ten

Opening the oven door, Dawn pulled out the rack and lifted the lid of the roasting pan. The rump roast was more than done; the meat was separating in chunks. She added a glass of water to try to keep it moist, turned the oven thermostat to warm, and slid it back into the oven.

"Boy, that smells good," Randy groaned in a complaining tone. "When are we going to eat? Do we have to wait until Dad comes home?"

In private, he'd taken to calling Slater "Dad," although it was done rather self-consciously when he was in his presence. Dawn felt Slater had been gone so much that his absence had contributed a lot to Randy's occasional unease with him.

"Don't you think we should wait?" she asked, appealing to his sense of right.

"It depends on how late he's going to be," Randy grumbled.

Breathing in deeply, Dawn had to concede that it wasn't an unfair condition. If they waited much longer, the meal would be ruined. She moved to the wall telephone.

"I'll call him and find out how soon he expects to be home. If he's going to be too late, we'll eat without him." She picked up the receiver and dialed the number.

It rang three times before it was answered. "MacBride." His curt voice sounded in her ear, its sharp, clipped tone becoming all too familiar to her.

"Are you still at the office?" she said, trying to sound light and amusing.

A heavy sigh came over the line, weary with exasperation. "I'm busy, Dawn. Why are you calling? If it's just to check up on me and make sure I'm not with someone else, then why don't you drive by my office and spare me these interruptions?"

She gritted her teeth and didn't respond to his biting sarcasm and irritation. "Randy's hungry. He wants to know what time you'll be home for dinner."

Instantly she was angry with herself for putting the onus of the call on their son. She was more interested in the answer than Randy was—and more deserving of an explanation for why they saw so little of him.

"It'll be late. Don't wait dinner for me. I'll send out for something to eat," Slater informed her that she needn't keep anything warm for him. "Tell Randy good night for me."

Which meant he wouldn't be home before eleven o'clock. "I'm beginning to feel like an abandoned bride," she laughed brittlely, because it seemed the best way to keep the tears at bay.

"Don't tell me Simpson never had to work late at the office," he chided unkindly.

"Not night after night," she shot back, her hand trembling from its tight grip of the receiver. Not caring how rude it was, she hung up the phone with a sharp click. She took a couple of seconds to regather her poise before turning to Randy. "He said not to wait dinner, so we can go ahead and eat."

"When's he coming home?" Without being told, Randy went to the cupboard to take down the plates and set the table.

"Not until very late. He said to tell you good night." There was an underlying threat of tautness in her otherwise light-sounding voice.

"Gosh," Randy sighed. "I thought it'd be different after you two got married and we all lived in the same house. But I'll bet I saw him more before you got married."

"He's been busy," she defended Slater's absence to Randy even if she had her own doubts about the necessity of it. "It won't always be like this."

"I hope not." His mouth twisted grimly as if he didn't have much hope things would change.

When they had first returned from their honeymoon, Dawn had been willing to concede that Slater had a lot of work that he needed to catch up on, so she had accepted his late nights without complaint. Sometimes she woke in the middle of the night and found him asleep in bed with her, but half the time she never heard him come home—or leave with morning's first light.

His attitude remained preoccupied, sometimes —like tonight—his lack of patience turned him sarcastic. Naturally with Randy, he was friendly and warm. Dawn was the one bearing the brunt of whatever was bothering him. She doubted that she could take much more.

On Sunday morning, Dawn could hardly believe it when she wakened at seven and discovered Slater had already risen. She hurried to the window and saw the Corvette in the driveway below. It seemed a rarity to discover he hadn't already left the house. She dressed hurriedly in a pair of white jeans and a red-checked blouse, applied a sparing amount of makeup, ran a comb through her hair, and ran down the stairs.

She found him in the living room, sprawled in an armchair with the sections of the Sunday newspaper strewn around him. His shuttered gaze flicked to her, then back to the article he was reading. A cup was sitting on the lampstand.

"Coffee?" She presumed it was made since the evidence seemed to indicate he'd already had at least one cup.

"I've had plenty. Thank you," he refused.

"I think I'll get myself a cup," Dawn announced unnecessarily and turned to leave the room.

The clumping thud of Randy running down the steps checked her as she waited for him to come down. When he was around, things didn't seem as tense.

"Good morning." He was always bright and

chipper in the mornings. "What's for breakfast?" And hungry.

"What would you like?" Dawn gave him his choice.

"Pancakes and sausage." Randy didn't have to think about it.

"Slater?" She turned to him. "The same for you?"

"No, I'm not hungry," he refused again. "I've already had some toast and juice."

"Say, Dad—" Randy sauntered over to the armchair where Slater was seated, "—can we go out on the boat today? You've been saying we would —one of these weekends."

"Not today." He folded the section of paper he'd been reading, laid it aside and reached for the next. "I have to go over to the resort later on. I'll be tied up most of the afternoon."

"Ah, not today, too," Randy complained.

"Surely you can take one day off," Dawn argued.

"If I didn't feel it was necessary, I wouldn't be spending my Sunday working," Slater countered. "The subject is closed."

The paper crackled as he snapped it open. Aware of Randy's crestfallen expression, Dawn curved a protective hand around his shoulder and turned him toward the kitchen.

"Let's fix some breakfast," she said.

Neither of them spoke as they walked to the kitchen. While Dawn put sausage links in the skillet to fry, Randy set the table. She took down the pancake flour to whip up a batch.

173

"Would you bring me the milk from the refrigerator—and an egg?" she asked.

The door opened and shut behind her while she measured out the mix. Randy appeared at her elbow, holding an egg. "There's no milk."

"I used the last of it last night," she remembered with a disgruntled sigh. "Bring me my purse. It's on the counter over there. You can ride your bike to the corner store and buy a quart." Randy started over to the side counter. "Wait," Dawn called him back. "I used the last of my cash to pay the paperboy. I'll get it from your father. Watch the sausage for me."

Wiping the pancake dust from her hands with a towel, Dawn walked swiftly into the front room. Slater was still engrossed in the paper.

"We're out of milk. I need to send Randy to the store to get some," she explained. "Will you give me some money? I'm broke."

There was a long, cool look from his gray eyes. Something like contempt touched his mouth as he reached into his pocket and pulled out a handful of bills. When she started toward his chair, he tossed them to her. They separated and drifted to the floor like green leaves settling to the ground.

"That's what you wanted, isn't it?" Slater challenged.

When she finally ripped her gaze away from the money at her feet, she glared at him. She made no move to touch it or pick it up.

"Hey, Mom! Should I—" Randy came running in from the kitchen.

"Go outside and play, Randy," she ordered.

"But—what about the milk?" He saw the bills scattered on the floor. "What's all that money doing there?"

"I said go outside and play!" Dawn repeated herself more sharply.

Randy backed up a step, looking from his mother to his father, finally sensing the explosive tension in the room. Then he wheeled, and headed for the front door. It slammed shut behind him. Dawn had a glimpse of him out the window, his arm hooked around a veranda pillar, his head hanging low as if his world had come to an end.

Her temper was trembling on the edge of fury as she knelt down and began picking up the money with false calm. "Would you mind explaining to me what *this* is all about?" She held up a wad of bills to indicate what she meant.

The newspaper was shoved aside, all pretense of reading it abandoned as Slater pushed to his feet. The hard angles of his features were whitened at the edges with barely controlled rage.

"No more games, Dawn," he snapped. "Don't pretend that isn't what you wanted when you know very well it is! Now you've got it."

"What are you talking about?" she demanded.

"I'm talking about you. You're probably going to turn out to be the most expensive lay in the country," he charged viciously. "Well, there's your money. Payment in full for your services. And enjoyable they were, too."

She straightened to stand erect, her head high

and hot tears stinging her eyes. "Just exactly what do you think I've done?" Her voice was strained with the effort to keep it level.

"I can't keep up this farce any longer," he sighed heavily. He was angry, but it was a tired kind of anger. Dawn could see the haggard and worn lines etched in his features from too many nights with too little sleep, but she couldn't feel sorry for him. "You married me for money. Well, now you've got it." Slater flung a gesturing hand in the direction of the money she held. "Sorry it isn't more than that, but I don't carry a lot of cash on me."

"Is that really what you believe?" Dawn asked with a hurt and incredulous frown. She breathed out a short laugh as she looked down at the money, her eyes blinking aside the tears. Events were becoming clear to her. "All this started that last night on the beach when I told you Simpson hadn't left me any money. I knew you had changed toward me, but I didn't know why."

"It was clever of you to wait until *after* we were married to mention that *little* detail," Slater said with dry sarcasm that seemed to mask his pain.

"The irony of this is that I was beginning to wonder if you were upset because you had married me for the money," she admitted her brief suspicion. "And you were angry because you hadn't allied yourself with wealth. I kept telling myself it was absurd, but I never dreamed you would come to this ridiculous conclusion."

"Is it so ridiculous?" he challenged. "Don't forget I know how much you wanted money. You threw *us* away to get your hands on it. When I think what a fool I've been, believing all that garbage about marrying again for love." He swung at right angles from her, running a hand over his hair and gripping the back of his neck. "I'm the one who's been saying it, then letting myself believe that it came from you."

"Love is the reason I married you," Dawn insisted.

"Love for me or love for money?" countered Slater.

"How can you even ask that question?" she demanded with the wad of money crumpled in her rigidly clenched fist. "We honeymooned together. Every minute of it was wonderful. Surely you could tell how much I love you."

"You've had so much practice faking your feelings that you probably wouldn't know a real emotion when it came your way." He shook his head in disgust, unimpressed by her show of evidence. "You played the loving wife for so long with Simpson, you probably don't know how to act any other way. He may have preferred the pretense, but I don't."

"Slater, don't you know that I never stopped loving you?" Dawn was at a loss as to how to convince him. There was a part of her that rebelled at the idea she had to try.

"Maybe I have trouble believing you ever loved me in the beginning," he replied with weary flatness. "If you loved me, how could you marry someone else?"

"What I did was wrong. I learned that very

quickly, but the damage had already been done."
She struggled with the unpleasant memories. "I
suppose it was wrong to stay married to Simpson
after I realized what a mistake I'd made. But I'd
made my bed and I thought I had to stay in it."

"It must have been a low blow when he didn't
leave you anything," Slater taunted.

"I didn't want anything!" Dawn flared.

"Contesting the will would have meant a long,
legal court fight, not to mention a very expensive
one. How much easier it was just to find yourself
a new sucker—me." His laughing breath was
loaded with self-derision. "I swore I wouldn't let
myself be fooled by you again. But you had me all
set up just right, didn't you? You had a hook
waiting for me no matter which way I went."

"No—"

But he didn't allow her to finish. "When Simpson died and you found out you were broke again,
you must have looked around for the most likely
candidate. And there was good ole MacBride.
You knew he had been crazy about you—and
there just might be some smouldering coals left
in him. He had become something of a success—
not filthy rich but on his way up. And the *coup de
grâce*, you had borne him a son, a little secret
you'd kept all this time."

"I should have told you. I've already admitted
that," she reminded him angrily. "I came back
here so the two of you could get to know one
another. And that's the only reason I came back!
It wasn't to trick you into marrying me so I could
get my hands on your money."

"You made me believe that once, but I won't be persuaded again," Slater declared with a long, heavy look. "If it means anything, I have finally come to terms with who and what you are. A leopard can't change her spots—and you are a cat of the first order." His gaze flicked to her flaming hair.

"How do you know she can't?" Dawn challenged. "Did you ever ask a leopard?"

"It's no use, Dawn." There was a hard finality in his voice. "You were right when you said a couple couldn't stay together because of a child. And I can't live your lie anymore."

"It isn't a lie," she insisted with cold anger. "But if you don't believe that, then you can't love me."

"It seems we've reached a fork in the road." He sounded calm, painfully so as far as Dawn was concerned.

"It seems we have." She tried to match him and strained for a cool nonchalance that kept wavering on bitterness. "You claimed to have urgent business to attend to, so why don't you go take care of it. I'll pack your things and have them sent to the boat this afternoon."

"Fine." There was a rigidness to his jaw.

"And I shan't be asking for any financial settlement from you," Dawn asserted. "If you feel you should contribute something to Randy's support, then follow your conscience and pay whatever you feel is fair."

"You're fighting right down to the last second, aren't you?" Slater accused tightly, a glint of reluctant admiration in his gray eyes. "It's a great gesture to subtly make me wonder whether I've been wrong about you all along."

That was too much for Dawn. She was shaking with rage. "Do you want another gesture?" she hurled. "Try this!" She pointed a rigid finger in the direction of the front door while she glared at him. "Get out!"

His long strides carried him past her and out the door. The glass rattled in the window panes from the force behind the slamming of the door. Dawn glared after him, hating him at that moment as passionately as she had ever loved him.

The roar of the sportscar reversing out of the drive finally broke her anger-stiffened stance. She turned away from the door and started to lift a hand to her forehead in angry despair. Her glance fell on the paper money of various denominations in her hand. Her fingers tightened on it, crushing it more.

"You think it's your money I want," she caustically informed an absent Slater. "I'll show you what I think of your money!"

Driven by an anger that cloaked a pain too excruciating to be exposed, Dawn swept across the room to the cypress-topped coffee table. She dumped the bills into the large glass ashtray sitting on it. She grabbed a matchbook and ripped out a cardboard match, striking it and holding the flame to the money.

It licked greedily at a corner, then jumped quickly from one paper bill to another. Soon the whole crumpled mass of wadded bills was consumed by fire. Dawn sank onto the edge of the couch to watch it burn with bitter satisfaction.

"That, Slater MacBride, is the grandest gesture of them all," she murmured with a twisted slant to her mouth.

As quickly as the fire had taken hold, it burned itself out. All that remained of the money were black strips of brittle ash. Yet a distinctly smoky smell continued to taint the air she breathed—like something scorched.

"The sausage!" She bolted for the kitchen.

She waved a hand at the smoke-filled air as she entered the room and hurried to the stove, coughing and choking from the smoke invading her lungs. Her eyes smarted. She had to keep blinking as she turned the burner off and slapped a lid on the smoking skillet. After switching on the overhead exhaust fan, Dawn ran around opening all the windows and fanning the air to hurry the smoke's departure.

With disjointed logic, she blamed it all on Slater. Of all times to start an argument, he had chosen when she was fixing Randy's breakfast. She would never have burned the sausages if it weren't for him. She went back to the stove to survey the damage.

"Gee, Mom." Randy came in the back door and stopped, wrinkling his nose at the burnt smell and wispy bits of smoke in the air. "What are you trying to do? Burn the place down?"

Dawn was too upset and angry to answer, but it was a question that didn't need an answer. When she lifted the lid of the skillet, there were four charred-black sticks encrusted in a sticky black mess of burned grease and sausage juice. She poked at the hard stuff with a spatula as Randy came over to take a look.

"Where'd Dad go in such a hurry?" Uncertainly, he peered sideways at her.

"He had business." The words were clipped short as she moved away from him to carry the skillet to the sink. Out of the corner of her eye, she noticed he'd left the back door standing open. "You forgot to close the door." It was an absent reprimand, too preoccupied with her own private turmoil.

"Did you and Dad have an argument?" Randy trailed after her to the sink, pausing just a little bit behind her.

"We disagreed on certain matters," Dawn replied stiffly, preferring to keep from her son how bitter the quarrel had been.

"You had a fight," he concluded with a sinking look. "Are you going to make up?"

"I don't know." She ran water in the skillet and stabbed viciously at the black crust.

"Is he coming back?"

"I don't know." Her voice became more clipped and more emphatic as she repeated the same answer.

"Are you going to get a divorce?"

"I don't know!" The word scraped over her strained nerves.

Dawn swung around to face him, angry with his hurting questions until she saw the frightened and lost expression on his young face.

Something crumpled inside her, letting all the pain and remorse through. The skillet and spatula were dropped in the sink as she reached for him.

"Randy, I'm sorry. I'm upset, but not with you," she assured him. "You aren't to blame for what's happened. You had nothing to do with it."

His head drooped, and she knew he was trying to hide his tears. "I wish I could help. I wish—" His emotionally taut voice didn't finish the sentence as he compressed his lips together to hold back a sob.

"Oh, Randy, you do help." Dawn cupped his cheek in her hand and turned his face up so she could see it. The loving stroke of her thumb wiped away the tear that had been squeezed out of his lashes. "You don't know how much I need you just to be with me. I hate to think what kind of selfish and self-centered person I might have become if you hadn't come into my life so I could finally learn the responsibilities that go along with loving someone," she explained. "You've been more help to me than you'll ever know. And even if you can't help solve the problems your father and I are having, just having you here makes it a little easier. Okay?" Her voice wavered on an emotional note as she forced an encouraging smile on her lips. Randy nodded a hesitant understanding and scrubbed a tear from his other cheek. "Then go close the door before you let in all the flies," she urged in an attempt to instill some reassuring normality to the scene.

Her hand slid off his cheek as Randy turned to

obey. Her gaze started to follow him, then leaped to the opened door where Slater was standing. There was a gentleness in his expression, a light in his gray eyes that seemed to be studying her for the first time.

"I heard what you told Randy," he said. "You weren't faking."

"That's big of you." Hurt, she swung away and gripped the edge of the sink an instant, then reached for the skillet to begin jabbing at the crust again. She shut her eyes briefly when she heard his footsteps approaching her.

"Will you listen to me?" Slater requested and started to turn her chin toward him with his hand. "I'm trying to tell you I was wrong."

Dawn jerked away from his touch and walked swiftly to the wall calendar by the phone to elude him. "I'd better mark that down." She picked up a pen and began writing on the date. " 'Today Slater MacBride said he was wrong.' There!" She flashed him a challenging look.

"I'm sorry," he insisted with persuasive sincerity. "What more do you want me to say? I misjudged you—your reasons—everything."

"I tried to tell you that but you twisted my words up and used them against me." Her anger was weakening but the deep hurt from his accusations wouldn't allow her to easily forgive him.

"I was wrong," Slater admitted again. "I realize that I was more willing to believe the worst than to trust you. I was scared of being hurt. It all seemed too good to be true so I tried to find something wrong with it. I let my suspicion feed n itself and never came to you with it. That was ny biggest mistake."

"And I should have told you about being eft out of Simpson's will from the start," she sighed, because the omission had eventually compounded the problem. "But I knew you'd take such delight in it," Dawn accused with a brief lash of her old fire.

"I probably would have," he agreed with a hint of a smile.

Randy watched them both cautiously. "Does his mean you aren't mad at each other anymore? You won't be getting a divorce?"

"Does it?" Slater quirked an eyebrow and silently appealed for her answer.

To be forgiven, one also had to be able to forgive. That was one of the responsibilities of loving. And she loved him. A smile slowly lifted the corners of her mouth as she held his gaze.

"Yes, that's what it means," she said softly.

As Slater started toward her, she came to meet him. Randy discreetly wandered to the window while they embraced, arms tightly holding each other. It was a rawly sweet kiss that healed the hurt they had inflicted on one another and gave birth to a stronger love. It shone in their eyes when the kiss ended and they gazed at each other.

Slater enfolded her more lovingly in his arms and nestled her head on his shoulder. They swayed slightly to the tempo of their fast-beating hearts. His hand rubbed over her hair in a caressing fashion.

"What I said about a leopard not changing her spots?" he murmured, tipping his chin down so he could have a glimpse of her face.

"Yes?" She glanced up, now able to wait for his explanation without jumping to a conclusion out of self-protection.

"They're born without spots and acquire them as they mature," he said.

He was blaming her youth for her actions all those years ago. She felt like crying out of sheer happiness because that tragic episode seemed finally behind them.

"Dad?" Randy had heard their murmuring voices and thought it safe to intrude on their conversation. "Where's your car? It isn't in the driveway."

Still holding Dawn, Slater turned his head to look at their son. "It's parked a couple of blocks away. I ran out of gas," he admitted with a wryly chagrined expression. "I meant to fill it last night and forgot."

"Why didn't you walk to the gas station and have the empty gas can in the trunk filled?" Randy frowned.

"There was a slight problem." He glanced down at Dawn, amusement glittering in his eyes. "I didn't have any money on me to pay for it. And the only station open on Sunday that's close by doesn't accept credit cards. So I had to come back to see if I couldn't persuade my wife to part with some of the money I'd given her. Do you suppose that could be arranged?"

"Oh, dear," she murmured. "I burned it all."

"You did what?" He drew his head back, eyeing her skeptically.

"I was mad so I put it in the ashtray and set fire to it," Dawn admitted.

There was a stunned moment of silence before Slater tipped his head back and laughed heartily. "What kind of woman did I marry?" he declared with a shake of his head. "She has to have money to burn."

"I'm sorry." It seemed so childish now.

"Living with you isn't going to be easy," he said.

"We'll make it," Dawn asserted confidently.

"Of course," Slater agreed. "You know what they say—the third time's a charm."

31